Choosing Life

In His Choosing
Book 1

By

Ronna M. Bacon

Colossians 3:23. Whatever you do, work at it with all your heart, as working for the Lord, not for human masters,

Isaiah 41:10. So do not fear, for I am with you; do not be dismayed, for I am your God. I will strengthen you and help you; I will uphold you with my righteous right hand.

Proverbs 14:27. The fear of the LORD is a fountain of life, turning a person from the snares of death.

Table of Contents

Chapter 1
Chapter 2
Chapter 3
Chapter 4
Chapter 5
Chapter 6
Chapter 7
Chapter 8
Chapter 9
Chapter 10
Chapter 11
Chapter 12
Chapter 13
Chapter 14
Chapter 15
Chapter 16
Chapter 17
Chapter 18
Chapter 19
Chapter 20
Chapter 21
Chapter 22
Chapter 23
Chapter 24
Chapter 25
Chapter 26
Chapter 27
Chapter 28
Chapter 29
Chapter 30
Chapter 31

Chapter 32
Chapter 33
Chapter 34
Chapter 35
Chapter 36
Chapter 37
Chapter 38
Chapter 39
Chapter 40
Chapter 41
Epilogue
Dear Readers

Rain teemed down outside in the early autumn day, becoming heavier and heavier as it fell. Rolling down the windows of the diner, it made it almost impossible for the patrons to see outside. Even though it was only around noon, the skies were as dark as evening.

Shifting on her bench seat, Shaye Connors felt danger approaching her. She had been out on her work day, heading for another call as an property estimator and had to pull in to avoid the heavy rain. Shaye had been uneasy that day, feeling as if she was followed but not seeing anyone around her. She sighed. Whatever or whoever it was? They had been dogging her path for months now and she wanted it over. She just didn't know who to turn to. Shaye had felt God's presence with her in a stronger way, particularly on that day.

Shaye looked up from where she had huddled in the corner of the booth and frowned at the tall handsome man who stood beside her seat, his mug of coffee in his hand as well as his utensils. She had no idea what he wanted but she didn't feel fear coming from him. She took in the dark auburn waves of his hair and the deep hazel eyes, eyes that held concern for her.

"I'm sorry, sweetheart. I didn't see you here." The man sat beside her, not close enough to worry or frighten her, just puzzle her. "My name's Slavin

O'Shea. I hope you don't mind that I join you. I have been watching you and watching a couple of men at the front of the diner. They are too interested in you." Slavin watched as Shaye closed her beautiful gray eyes and noted the unruly red curls. "Did I say something wrong?"

Shaye paused as their food was set in front of them, surprised to find Slavin reaching for her hand and then asking a blessing on their meal. She had not expected that.

"No, it's okay. I'm Shaye Connors. Thank you for your kindness. I have felt followed for months now, particularly today. I just didn't know who to turn to." Shaye stared down at her plate of fish and chips, not particularly hungry any more. "I didn't know who to turn to." She repeated herself, trying to convince herself that she really did need someone to turn to. Right now, that someone seemed to be the man sitting beside her.

"For now? Let me be that one." Slavin suddenly had no desire for this beautiful lady to walk out of his life. He gazed around at the patrons, seeing there were not that many, not as many as he had thought. His attention turned to the kitchen, not seeing many staff in there. But then, this was an out of the way diner that he had found as the rain had become heavier.

Shaye stared at him, not sure that she had heard him correctly.

"What did you just say?" Her voice held her puzzlement.

"I said, let me be the one you turn to." Slavin grinned at her before he bit into his hamburger. "This is good. Eat and then we'll pray. It looks as if the rain is lasting for a while. It's not in me to let a beautiful lady be in fear and on her own if I can prevent it." Slavin didn't continue and state that his work as an archivist had him seeing the dark side of life too much. He wanted better suddenly for Shaye.

Shaye shrugged, not sure if she should stay there but there wasn't really any option for her. She stared down at her meal, suddenly not all that hungry but knowing that she should eat. Shaye picked away at her food, fully aware of Slavin sitting beside her. She shivered suddenly, feeling evil in the room. She had always been able to do that. Shaye had prayed for that awareness to be removed but God had not done that. He had only increased how she was aware of evil and sin.

"Are you okay?" Slavin slanted a glance at her and then studied the patrons once more. He sighed. There were more than those two men. He could see another two men sitting near them who seemed too interested in Shaye. He began to pray, asking or rather, begging God to protect the lady with him and to show him how to get her out of the diner. That didn't seem to be happening, not at the moment. The rain was still heavy and he could hear the thunder cracking overhead and saw the sharp, bright flashes of lightning.

Shaye shook her head, afraid to speak. She began to pray, begging God for protection. She knew that He was there with them. Only, sometimes, He allowed things to happen. This particular situation that she found herself in? That seemed to be one of those occasions.

"No, I don't think that I am." Shaye sighed. "A friend dropped me off down the road as I wanted to walk the trails and didn't want my car sitting here. I'm to call her when I'm ready to go home." She peered out the window, not seeing much because of the darkness. "It's so dark, Shaye. And I am afraid. I don't know why or who is causing it."

Shaye nodded, knowing that he had read her correctly. Someone was after her and he would not allow her to walk through whatever it was on her own. It was not his character. Besides, working as he did with the local police department, he had friends who could help.

"I work with the local police. Once we're out of here, if you want, I can find a detective friend of mine and see what he has to say." Slavin kept his eyes on his empty plate before he shoved it away, looking up and nodding as the server held up the coffee pot. He might as well have another coffee. They weren't going anywhere any time soon.

"You would do that? You don't know me!" Shaye was shocked at that.

"No, I don't know you but I would like to consider you a new friend." Slavin grinned at her before he sobered. "And I would do that. None of my friends like to see ladies in trouble without moving in to help them."

Slavin looked up as he sensed movement in the room that had not been there moments earlier. He frowned as he watched the four men on their feet, moving around the area. He sighed, fear growing in his heart as he watched one man lock the doors and hear sounds of dismay and fear coming from the kitchen before the staff were herded into the eating area and made to sit.

Shaye gripped Slavin's arm, her fear rising.

"Slavin? What are they doing?" Shaye kept her voice as low as she could.

"Moving everyone into one spot. They want something or someone. I just pray that it's not you." Slavin continued to monitor the men, memorizing as much about them as he could. He had always had a good memory for faces and details and knew that God had placed him there, in the diner, at that time just for Shaye.

"Who?" Shaye moved closer to Slavin, not liking the looks that were being shot her way.

"Shaye? I'm going to ask you something. Do you have a boyfriend, husband, significant other?" Slavin kept his voice as low as he could, sensing Shaye shaking her head. "I don't either. I think, for now to protect you, we need to pretend that we are dating. Can you do that for me?" Slavin was not one to date, waiting for God to reveal the lady from his dreams. Right now? That lady was Shaye.

Shaye hesitated before she nodded, feeling Slavin's arm around her, drawing her closer to him. She frowned for a moment and then felt a sense of safety and protection from how he was holding her.

—

11

She just prayed that he was not hurt because he stepped in.

Chapter 2

Watching as the men paced around the perimeter of the room, Slavin tried to determine just what their game was as it could be put. He was afraid for Shaye. He felt his phone vibrating but didn't dare pull it out. His arm tightened around Shaye as the men seemed to keep her in their view.

"What do they want, Slavin?" Shaye was watching them as well, not sure how to respond to either them or Slavin.

"I don't know, Shaye. And we're stuck here for the duration." Slavin was looking around, trying to determine the best way to get Shaye, himself, and everyone else out of the diner. There just didn't seem to be a way. Besides, God had not given him permission to try anything or to walk away. He had learned early in life that he needed to obey those commands from God, even if it was just an impression. "We'll get out somehow, Shaye. I just worry about you."

"You're worried about me? You just met me!" Shaye was dismayed but also heartened at his words. Finally, she thought, someone to step in. "I don't know why someone would be following me. And that scares me."

"I know that it will. Let's just wait for a moment and then I might have a plan." Slavin watched the men closer, seeing the way that they were moving. They

———

13

were waiting for someone or something and that wasn't happy. That was making them uneasy. And uneasy bad guys as his brother would put it were unpredictable.

"Let me know when you come up with something." Shaye leaned against Slavin, not realizing that she was. Her attention was on the men as well. She didn't recognize them but then again, she didn't have a lot of contact with men other than if they were present when she did her home appraisals.

Slavin was on his feet for a moment, heading for the kitchen. He reached for the coffee pots and then walked around the diner, refilling the coffee mugs and offering tea if that was preferred. He knew full well that he was living dangerously by doing this but at the moment, his main concern was trying to determine just what the men were up to and who they were after. The rain was not easing off enough for him to try to escape. And that was exactly what he was determined to do.

Shaye was watching the men and the other patrons and staff. They all seemed to be waiting for something to happen and whatever that was, it didn't happen. She was on her feet, moving away from her seat and towards the facilities. These were located in a small hallway. She sensed one of the men moving to watch her before she shoved open the door. He turned away, not seeing Slavin walking quickly towards her.

Slavin waited for Shaye to open the door and then reached for her hand, rushing her towards the outside door. He opened it quickly and then ran for his car, Shaye keeping step with him. Once inside, Slavin sat for a moment, not sure if he had made the right move. His phone was out as he made the cal that he had never dreamed that he would have to, asking for help in a hostage situation.

The rain had eased somewhat, to the point that Slavin could see the diner. He looked around, knowing that if he drove away, that would be dangerous and might even cause the men to react violently to the staff and patrons inside the building.

"Slavin? Are we not leaving?" Shaye was puzzled by how Slavin was just sitting there.

"No, I don't have God's permission to do so. There is help on the way." Slavin reached into his back seat, finding the rain slickers that he had thrown in that morning. "Here. Put this on. Then, we'll find somewhere to hide. I don't want to drive away. They'll count the cars."

"But they know that we aren't in there anymore." Shaye stabbed a slim forefinger towards the diner. There was fear and anger both in her voice.

"I know that, Shaye. Just be patient for a moment." Slavin shrugged into his slicker and then was out of his vehicle, rounding the front to pull Shaye with him. He ran towards the forest that had encroached the area, tugging Shaye with him. He stopped as he entered the trees, searching for an area to hide in.

Sudden yells from outside the diner had both of the couple spinning to stare that way. Slavin desperately sought somewhere that he could at least hide Shaye. He shoved her towards a group of bushes and into the midst before he just stood, watching as two of the men walked towards him.

"Where is she?" The smaller of the men was not waiting for Slavin to respond. Instead, the bat that he had somehow retrieved was suddenly launched at Slavin, hitting him directly in the abdomen with violent force and sending him flying backwards to the ground. Slavin didn't move, his eyes closed even as pain crossed his face.

The two men stared at each other and then around the forest. They were city men and could face the meanest, most violent person on the city. In the country? That was a whole different ballgame for them, they decided, before they ran back towards the diner. They slid to a halt as they were confronted by the red and blue flashing lights of the emergency vehicles. Forced to move forward, they were shoved towards a patrol vehicle. Hands on the trunk of it, they were searched, their personal effects dropped to the trunk and then handcuffed before being shoved into separate vehicles.

The officers turned, eyes narrowing as they looked back at the men and then from the direction that they had run from.

"Slavin's here. He's not in the diner. Where is he?" John, a friend of Slavin's, was worried about him.

"You don't think…" Edward's voice died away before he was running towards the forest, heading for where the men had appeared.

"Let's hope not. We have paramedics?" John shot a look behind him.

"We do." Edward slid to a halt as he heard a female voice, clogged with tears, begging Slavin to awaken. "Who's that?"

"I don't know. Someone in the diner said a lady disappeared at the same time as Slavin. She was under the impression that they were a couple." John was puzzled at that.

"He's not dating anyone that we know of, is he?" Edward approached slowly, his eyes on Shaye and then on Slavin. "Slavin?"

Shaye jumped in fear as she hear other voices, convinced the men had returned and found them. She looked up, not taking in for a moment that there were police officers standing beside her, one bending over Slavin. He looked up at Shaye, seeing the raw fear on her face.

"Miss? What happened? Do you know?" Edward waited patiently for Shaye to respond. John had headed back to where the paramedics had arrived, motioning one of the teams to come with him.

"I don't know. Slavin hid me and then I heard a loud voice. The men disappeared. I waited for a few moments before I found Slavin. How bad is he?" Shaye was really worried and it was coming through in how fast that she was speaking.

"I don't know. We have paramedics that will assess him. Are you okay?" Once more, Edward waited for Shaye to respond. When she didn't, he looked up at John, whose hand was under her arm to draw her to her feet, despite her protests.

Chapter 3

Slavin roused slowly that evening, a hand to his abdomen. He had no idea what he had gone and done. All he knew was that he hurt. He felt a hand on his and reached to grasp it. It was a lady's, that much he knew.

His eyes opening slightly, Slavin stared around. A hospital room? He couldn't figure out why he was there. His head turned slightly as he stared at the beautiful lady watching him.

"I'm sorry. Do I know you?" Slavin had to clear his throat to be able to speak.

"You do. I'm Shaye. We were in a diner earlier and you helped to get me out. Only you were hurt." Shaye blinked back tears as she told him that.

Slavin looked past her as the door to the room opened and his brother, Sean, appeared. Sean frowned at Slavin before he turned to Shaye. Shaye simply stared back at him, not sure who he was.

"Sean?" Slavin's voice drew Shaye's attention back to him.

"Slavin? What did you do? John reached out to me as we got home from our trip." Sean frowned at his brother, his eyes on the hand that still gripped Shaye's.

"I was out at Mel's diner. This beautiful lady was in danger and I stepped in." Slavin didn't say anything more about that. "I just don't know why I'm here."

"From what John has said, you were attacked in the forest. They have arrested the men, but they're not talking." Sean was not surprised at that.

"No, they never do, do they? When can I leave?" Slavin was determined to leave that very night and then find a way to protect Shaye. He just didn't know how that would work.

"Tomorrow morning, Slavin. I'm here for the night. Now, your lady? Introduce me." Sean grinned at her.

"This is Shaye Connors." Slavin refused to let go of her hand. "She's in danger, Sean. I don't know why but we need to find out."

Shaye stared at him in disbelief. There was no way that was happening. She would be on her way and that would be it.

"You're not walking away from me. I won't let you." Slavin swung his feet off the bed. He was still dressed in the clothes, as muddy and damp as they were. "Sean? We're leaving. I'm not staying where we can be found. And you can bet that the men are out of jail and looking for us."

On his feet, Slavin simply reached for Shaye's hand. His body was aching badly and his head felt as if a dozen drummers had take up residency there. It would not stop him from leaving.

Sean shook his head and then followed his brother and the lady who seemed to be captivating Slavin's interest. He pointed to his vehicle, not sure where Shaye would end up but he hazarded a guess that it would be wherever Slavin was for the night.

"Slavin? We're heading for my place. Annie will want to mother you seeing as Mom and Dad are away. Shaye? That means that you come too. Slavin will not rest unless you are where he is. I know that for a fact." Sean just grinned at his brother's glare before he was shoving both of them into his car. He just shook his head as Slavin joined Shaye in the back seat, reaching for her hand despite her tugging it away from his tight grip.

Annie looked round as she heard Sean's voice, puzzled that he was home so soon. She saw Slavin and a young lady walking towards their kitchen. She sighed. Here we go, don't we, Lord? Slavin is attracted to a lady who is in danger or is it that Slavin is in danger? We need to figure this out and fast.

"Slavin? Should you be home?" Annie hugged her brother-in-law and then surprised Shaye by hugging her. "Shaye? May I call you that? You'll want to get cleaned up. Here, come this way. I think I have some clothes that will fit." Annie walked away with Shaye, not seeing the look that she was throwing back at Slavin.

Slavin watched Shaye walk away before he turned to Sean, finding his brother trying had to hold back his grin.

"You think this is funny?" Slavin had trouble controlling his own smile.

"I do. You used to tease me about Annie. It's your turn now." Sean reached to hug his brother. "I'm glad that you're okay. I was so worried when John called." He reached to place a plate of food on the table for Slavin, knowing full well that Slavin would want to clean up. "Here. Slavin. You can eat after you clean up." He reached to draw Slavin to his feet and then to another of their spare rooms. "Annie's set out some clothes for you. Are you okay on your own?"

Sean's quiet question and concern had Slavin blinking rapidly. They were close as brothers but this? This had put into play something that neither one of the brothers had ever experienced. They had no way of knowing what Slavin would be facing or what Shaye would either. For now, all Sean could do was pray for his brother and his lady.

John walked back towards the diner. He was puzzled by what had taken place. No one had been able to fully explain what had happened or why the men had tried to abduct either Shaye or Slavin. That was a part of the investigation now. John had been pulled in by the detective to aid him. John wanted to take the open slot on that squad and had applied for it. He had just not heard if that would happen.

"Edward? Do we have a sense of what happened or why?" John turned to his fellow officer.

"No, we don't. Slavin hasn't been able to say much. He's not remembering a lot. And that is about what we expected, isn't it?" Edward was frustrated as well.

"We should have some sort of sense." John signed. It was going to be a long night. They had finally managed to obtain all the witness statements

and send the people on their way. They had also
arranged for Slavin and Shaye's vehicles to be towed
to their respective homes.

———

23

A week later, Slavin was no further ahead in his search to know why his assault had happened or who they were really after. That frustrated him to no end. Even as he went about his normal duties and activities, the reason why was not far from his mind. Slavin had tried to contact Shaye. That lady just was not responding to his voice mails or test messages and that concerned him.

Walking into their church that morning, Slavin looked around, seeing Shaye sitting by herself at the back of the sanctuary. He hesitated before he stood beside her, waiting for her to respond. When she didn't look up or at him, he simply sat beside her and then reached for her hand.

Shaye jumped as she felt a hand on hers. She looked up, her eyes round with fear as she stared at Slavin. Of course he would have to be there, wouldn't he, she thought. She had been ignoring all of his messages, not sure how to respond to him. Shaye had to admit that he had taken a beating in all likelihood for her. She just wasn't sure how to respond to that or if she even should.

"Shaye? Are you okay?" Slavin's vice was quiet as he spoke, the sound hushed under the bustle and noise of the pre-service greetings.

Shaye shrugged. She wasn't sure how to feel or if she was okay.

"I don't know. How are you?" Shaye watched him closely, seeing as he shrugged off her concern. That angered her. She was on her feet and walking away from him, heading for the door.

Slavin stood with a hand on the top of his head before he was almost running after her. Today, it was more important that he find her and discuss what happened than to be in church. Their minister, Josiah, would understand completely.

"Shaye? Wait!" Slavin stopped her with a hand to her arm. He watched as she refused to look at him. "What just happened?"

"What just happened?" Shaye spun to stare at him. "What just happened? I asked how you were. You just shrugged off a question that needs to be answered."

Neither of the couple saw John watching them, an amused smile on his face for a moment before he moved in to stand almost between them. He wasn't sure what had happened but he could feel the sense of danger approaching them both.

"Slavin? Shaye? Should you two be standing out here in the open?" John watched as they continued to glare at one another. "Come on, you two. Into your vehicles and let's leave. We need to talk and talk now." John didn't give the couple an option, turning them both towards where they were parked and watching as they drove away, one after the other, with him following them.

Parking at a nearby coffee shop, John watched the couple once more. They were a couple, he decided, whether they had admitted that to themselves or not. And it was up to him at that point to get through to them that they were in more danger than they thought.

Sliding onto a booth seat, Shaye watched as Slavin sat beside her, waiting for John to return with their orders. She was very uncomfortable at that moment, more than a little afraid for Slavin and his family. The messages that she had been receiving had been that nasty as she phrased it.

John slid the tray onto the table top and then bowed his head. They needed to pray and pray hard. For now, that seemed to be the only and the best option that they had.

"John? You wanted to speak with us?" Slavin didn't look away from Shaye as he spoke. She was avoiding looking at him, staring out of the window instead.

"I do. And Shaye, you do need to listen. It is known around town that someone is after both of you. We don't have the understanding or information yet as to why. And the people on the street are looking for that for us." John didn't mention that there were undercover officers doing just that.

"I am listening, John. I just don't have to like it." Shaye was digging in her heels. She had never been threatened before and was just so afraid. She pulled out her phone and found the messages that she had received before she gave John her phone. "I've been getting these in the last day. Who is doing this?"

Slavin reached for her hand, his tightening on hers as she tried to pull it away. She frowned at him, seeing a look in his eyes that said that she was important to him and that he was worried about her. Shaye then turned her attention to their hands, seeing that he was just not letting go of her and that indeed puzzled her.

John shook his head, his smile not quite hidden. These two were dancing around each other, attracted to one another, and not sure how to proceed. That was so unlike his friend, Slavin, who was usually very decisive and sure of what he wanted and how to proceed.

"Shaye? Are these all that you've received?" John's low voice brought Shaye's attention back to him.

"They are. They're to my work phone. I don't have my personal number out there, only to friends." She sighed. "And both of you want that, don't you?"

"We do, Shaye. We need a way to reach you when you're not working. I am assuming that you don't answer your work phone outside of hours?"

Shaye shook her head, knowing that John was correct in what he asked.

"I don't. I have made that a habit, knowing that I needed downtime from work. At one time, I didn't and was burning out." She sighed heavily. "And just who would be after me? And why? Or is it Slavin that they're after? Slavin, just what do you do any way for work?"

Slavin grinned at her. They had never discussed their work but he had done an internet search on Shaye and realized just how much she would be out there on her own.

"I'm an archivist. For the most part, I work with conservation groups but I also work with the police department when they need to research old files or documents. That's part of who I am. And that could mean that someone was after me, for seeing something in one of those files." Slavin paused before he continued. "You mentioned that you're an estimator? How much are you out there?" He shared a look with John.

"A lot. I go into homes and onto properties to estimate their value. I do this by myself. I don't work for a certain company. Not many of us do. But that has to change, doesn't it? I can't put myself out there on my own. That sucks, you know."

Both men grinned at her phrasing of how she felt and both agreed with her.

"No, I don't think that you can, Shaye. For now, I have a list of officers who are willing to help you out when you need to be out there." John slid a folded piece of paper across the table to her. "Use it. I don't want to explain to anyone that you refused and ended up disappearing or dead. We don't want to lose you as a friend in that way."

Shaye stared at him, her eyes wide with shock. This was not what she had expected. She had expected him to tell her that she needed to quit her work. And she wasn't ready to do just that.

Chapter 5

Slavin waited patiently for Shaye to decide to head towards her car. She just stood there, lost in thought. He shared a look with John before he reached for her hand. Shaye jumped as he did so, surprise on her face.

"Come on, Shaye. Let's get you out of here. We need to do that." Slavin simply grinned at her before he was moving her away from where they had been standing. He was not surprised, somehow, that they had managed to park side by side. And John was parked beside Shaye's car.

"How about that?" John grinned at the two. "God arranged our parking this morning." He hesitated while they were still a number of feet from their cars, his hand coming out to stop them. "Wait a sec. Let me check out the cars first." John walked away, intent on doing that.

Shaye frowned at Slavin, not sure what John was up to before she sighed. They were taking care of her and she wasn't sure how she felt about that. God seemed to be working that way, she thought, and then shrugged.

"Why is he doing that? You wanted us to leave? Now, we're not?" Shaye glared at Slavin before her attention went to John and how he was walking around the cars and then disappearing from sight.

"He's searching them, Shaye, for anything that doesn't belong. You know, like tracking devices, flat tires, bombs." He wasn't watching Shaye as he spoke, his own attention on John.

"Bombs?" Shaye slapped a hand across her mouth. "Did you really say bombs?" She wasn't quite sure that she had heard him, but the air was clear and crisp, the sounds of nature in her ears along with the faint sounds of traffic and then the music from inside the diner.

Slavin's head swung around as he stared at her, before he nodded. Apparently, Shaye had not thought of that.

"I did say bombs. We have to search our vehicles now until this is resolved." He grinned at the glare that Shaye directed towards the cars. "It's not their fault, Shaye."

"No, it's not. I want this over yesterday." She tugged her hand from Slavin's grasp and wrapped her arms around herself before she began to pace in what limited space that he would allow her. "Who is doing this?"

"We don't know yet, Shaye. The investigation is only starting. It might take months." Slavin grinned to himself once more at she spun and then stomped towards him. "No? Don't like that?"

"No, I most certainly do not. It can't take months. I can't live with the restrictions for that long." Shaye looked around, ready to run before she screamed.

Slavin spun as he heard her scream and then heard the sound of a motor rushing their way. He wrapped her into his arms and threw them sideways, knowing that he didn't have time to run with her to safety. The hot air of the motor shot towards them even as the car headed their way. He rolled them towards a nearby truck and under it, an arm coming up to cover their heads.

The car swerved at the last moment, shooting gravel at them that pelted them in a hard manner before it shot around and out of the parking lot. John was running their way, his phone out to call it in. He just didn't know if he had managed to capture what information was needed.

On his knees, he bent over to stare at Slavin who was staring back at him in shock. A hand reached out to his friend and his lady, to pull them to safety. Slavin was on his feet, leaning against the truck, his arms tight around Shaye. Shaye hid her face against him, shaking with her fear. This should not be happening, she decided. Not at all. She spun to glare at John, whose attention was on tracing where the car had come from and where it had disappeared to.

Sean had come looking for his brother, stopping short of where Slavin stood before Slavin shook his head.

"Slavin?" Sean leaned his back against the truck, not sure what to say or what to ask.

"Someone just tried to run us down. They would have succeeded if Shaye had not been facing that way and saw them. God was here and protected us." Slavin could not continue, his emotions rolling over and over. It had been too close.

<hr>

Shaye shoved away from Slavin, walking towards her car. She was in it and driving away before John could stop her. She needed to be safe and for her, that safety at the moment was her home. She didn't feel safe anywhere, really, not any more. Who would have thought that someone would try to run them down at a church? Who did that kind of stuff anyways? Shaye sighed to herself. She had run and shouldn't have. She didn't know if her car was even safe. She had just followed her instincts to hide.

John watched as Shaye drove away, his phone out to request that an officer be at Shaye's home, preferably a female officer who could be inside with that lady until he could reach out to her. He turned as he heard footsteps and saw officers moving in on them.

"Slavin? Are you two okay? I know. I know. Shaye took off and should not have." John stopped beside his friends.

"I think so. I want this person, John. This is personal. And I want to know why. Who did we anger or is it about someone else and we're being used to get to that person?" Slavin was thinking aloud, not really following his own thought trail.

John stared at him before he nodded. That was something that he was discussing with the other detectives. He had made that squad and had been paired with the older detective, Jerome, who was investigating this crime against Slavin and Shaye.

"We don't know that yet, Slavin. We don't have the information that we need. And we will get it. I promise you that."

"Yeah, I know that you will. Only who gets hurt in the meanwhile." Slavin looked towards his car. "I can't leave with my car, can I?"

"No, you can't. There is an interesting package sitting under it. I have techs on the way. How be you head off with Sean? I'll track you down." John shared a grin with Sean. "Go find your lady. Calm her down. I need to find her as well." He walked away with a wave, heading for where he saw Jerome approaching.

"Did he just say that?" Slavin stared after him.

"Say what?" Sean's hand on Slavin's arm was directing him towards his car. Annie had not been there that morning, fighting a headache and just needing to stay out of the noise, although welcome noise, from church.

"That she's my lady? That's not happening." His words belied his hopes and dreams. Shaye was exactly the image of who he had been praying for all those years.

Chapter 6

Pausing as she turned on the coffee pot, Shaye's head spun as she heard the doorbell. She never had visitors. Walking carefully that way, she stared out of the window to the right of the door. Of course, he would show up and he brought reinforcements. Could she pretend not to be at home? The doorbell ran again, causing Shaye to sigh before she reached for the lock and pulled open the door.

Slavin stared at her before he moved in to hug his lady. She stood for a moment before she was hugging him back.

"Slavin? What are you doing here? And you brought your brother!" Shaye struggled to release herself, backing slightly away from the two men before she turned. "In the kitchen. I just put on coffee. And I have sandwich stuff." She blinked back tears. Someone was trying his best to take care of her. That was something that she had prayed for, never expecting it to ever happen.

"It's okay, Shaye. We just needed to make sure that you were safe." Slavin stood at the table, his hands gripping the back of a chair. He watched as Sean moved around the kitchen, following the silent pointing that Shaye was doing to find what he needed.

"And you couldn't just phone?" Shaye spun to face him before she sighed once more. "I'm sorry. This has not been a good day in a not so great week. Sit and eat." She set the plates of food on the table in a careful manner, not slamming them down in anger as she so wanted to do.

"No, it has not been a good week for any one of us." Slavin reached to shove Shaye's chair into the table before he was seated beside her, a hand reaching for hers as Sean prayed. Looking up, he caught his brother's eyes, shaking his head slightly.

Sean nodded, having picked up the fact that Shaye was deeply terrified. It was more than just fear. And he wanted to know why as it affected his brother. And anything that affected his brother affected him and Annie.

Their meal finished and the plates stacked in the sink, Sean sat once more, his eyes on his folded hands before he looked up and then bowed his head once more. He began to pray, bringing in every verse that he could think of that meant safety, comfort, peace, protection. Slavin picked up the prayer when Sean finished. He knew only too well that God was the only One who could and would truly protect them.

"Shaye?" Sean shared look with Slavin as he spoke. "What have you discovered?"

"What have I discovered?" Her voice rose as she asked that question. "I haven't discovered anything. Have you?" She was becoming combative, fear driving that.

"No, we haven't and we should." Slavin's hand went up to still her words. "John is working it for us along with Jerome. He has questions that he will need to ask over and over. It's how it goes, Shaye. I don't like it any more than you do. This is compounding danger and fear in our lives and that's not how we are to live." He dropped his head, struggling to control both his fear for Shaye and his family and also his anger. He had had it out with God the night before, laying those two emotions before him. Only, as a human, they were rearing their ugly heads once more and he knew he would be back on his knees to fight it out once more.

"I get that, Slavin. I truly do. I don't like looking over my shoulder no matter where I am, to see if someone is coming after me. And they are. I've forwarded on increasing vile text messages to John. He can't trace them, he tells me. And if he can't trace them, then he can't find out who it is and stop them." Shaye blinked rapidly, tears clouding her vision. "I want this over. You need to go on with your own life and so do I." Her voice had dropped to a whisper, barely audible to the two men.

Slavin gave a faint sound and then was up from his chair and kneeling on the white and gray cushion flooring beside Shaye, his arms wrapping around her. He bowed his head as he prayed for his lady, acknowledging once more that was how he thought of her.

Sean was on his feet, heading for the door, having heard a soft tap at it. He frowned as he studied the man standing there, not recognizing him.

"Can I help you?" Sean didn't open the door all the way, bracing his foot against it and keeping a hand on the door knob.

The man looked up, nodding. Sean was taking precautions as he well should. His identification was out.

"My name is Peter. I have a security team in this town. John reached out to me, asking if I would speak with you and Shaye, is it?" He waited for Sean to respond.

"You mean my brother, Slavin. I'm Sean." Sean stepped outside and waited for a moment, seeing John walking towards them. "How do you know John?"

"He's my cousin. He has done this before. John?" Peter turned as John stopped beside him. "Where are we meeting? And who all is involved?"

John grinned at his cousin before he turned to Sean, assessing that man. He could tell that Sean was struggling as well, trying to make sense of what was going on with his brother.

"Sean? Where are Slavin and Shaye?" He continued to grin as he saw Shaye peeking out from behind Sean. "Shaye?"

"John? Why are you here?" Shaye shook her head and then headed back towards the kitchen, walking into Slavin's hug.

The three other men stared at one another before they followed her and greeted Slavin.

"Shaye? Peter has a security team. He is here to provide information that you and Slavin might need to stay safe. And it is up to you if you follow his advice or not." John was not backing down from them at all, needing to have that conversation with them both. He was glad that they were together and they would only have to do it one time. Or at least, that was what he hoped.

Chapter 7

Shaye simply stared back at John and then at Peter. She could sense that Slavin was waiting for her to respond. Only, she couldn't say a word. What could she say that would change what had happened? God was allowing it for some reason and she had to trust Him. That trust was hard to come by some days.

"Okay, Shaye. Slavin. As I said, Peter has a security team. We need to hear what he has to say. If you don't listen to him, then I know of at least three other teams that I can approach." John waited somewhat impatiently for either one of the couple to respond. And they were a couple, John decided, whether they acknowledged that or now.

"I see. What would you suggest then, Peter?" Slavin finally spoke, a hand resting on Shaye's, stilling the restless movement of hers.

"This is what I would recommend. John has expressed his concern about you two and what you faced and may face. This is not unusual for our forces and our teams to work together." Peter slid a stapled pile of papers over in front of both Slavin and Shaye. "Of course, we have no idea as of yet why you faced what you did or who is even after you. That's where John and the team of detectives will work and uncover it. We do have resources that we can go to if we need to. I suspect that we will." He waited for either of them to respond, sharing a look with John. "Once more, it is up to you whether you go along with what we may need to do. If you don't, it may well mean your death, the death of a family member or friend, or the death of an innocent bystander. These men have shown that they really don't care how, when or where that they approach you. It is your choice. I pray that you will at least listen to what we have to say."

Slavin was nodding. He was well aware of what could transpire. His gaze shifted to Shaye, finding her attention on the paperwork. Slavin looked down at the papers and then was lost in reading them, not really surprised at the concise and precise wording of what Peter was laying out. He knew somewhat of what he did, just from his friendship with John.

Shaye rested her head on her upraised hand, frowning at what she was reading. She sighed to herself and then began to pray, begging God to remove her from this danger. She wasn't ready to go through anything, not at all. Looking up at last, Shaye studied first John and then Peter before she was on her feet, to pace around the kitchen.

John kept an eye on her before he stood, stepping into her path and making her stop. He frowned at the look in her eyes. She was scared, he decided, and trying hard to figure out how to escape without any further harm coming to Slavin. That, John knew, would likely not happen.

"Shaye? Talk to me. Tell me what you are thinking." John was not backing down from her, not one bit, knowing that he had to have her input.

"What do I think? I think that I need to pack up and move. That's what I think." Her words were bit out in anger and also fear.

<hr>

"That won't work, Shaye. If they are after you and it seems that they are, they would only follow you. That increases your danger and the danger to those around you. Besides, if you live, they may well go after Slavin to make you return. Can you live with the fact that he may be more seriously hurt to get to you?"

Shaye's eyes met Slavin's, seeing a look in them that had her frowning. She shook her head. She could not choose to move, not when it was put that way. She could, however, choose life and that was the decision that she had arrived at during her pacing. God didn't want her to live in fear or hiding.

"I choose life, John. How do we do this then? I have to be out and about with my work. I can't take someone with me every time I go into a home or onto a property to do an assessment." Shaye's hands were waving at him. "I know. It's too dangerous not to have someone." Shaye blinked back tears. "I just don't have that kind of support."

"We know, Shaye. We know. That's why we want you to work with us. Peter's team can help. If you need to go out and do an assessment, he'll be with you or one of his five team members will. Our friends will help. I have offers from officers to go with you, either in uniform or on their own time. You are not alone in this. Never again will you be alone." John pointed a finger at Slavin, who was watching their conversation with interest on his face. "And I know that Slavin will be with you when he can. Please. Come and sit back down."

Shaye finally nodded, finding her chair once more. She looked down at Slavin's hand as it covered hers before she looked over at Peter. A frown once more covered her face.

"Peter? I think that you have an idea that I may not like."

Peter simply grinned at her before he handed over a single sheet of paper.

"I do. For now, we would suggest that you two act as a couple. Go out and about together. Go out for meals, walks, to church, just shopping. I know it's not what you would suspect to hear from us, but if you two stay hidden and apart, this will never end." Peter watched with compassion as Shaye's eyes closed and a single tear trickled down her cheek. "It's hard, Shaye, facing what you are. I have a number of friends that I can put you into contact with. That list that I just handed you? Those are some of them. Three of the security teams in the area have faced danger in their personal lives. We want to see that not happen to you but as realists, we know that it will. Work with us, that's all we're asking."

Shaye finally nodded, watching as Slavin's hand tightened on hers once more. It would be dangerous for them both. She just didn't know if she could live with herself if something happened to anyone because of her. Shaye was too much of a realist as well to not know that danger was around them.

Walking through his home late that night, Slavin was puzzled. Shaye had agreed to date him for the interim, not that she seemed to really want to but she would. He wanted more than that. She was a lady whom he was interested in dating for real, without danger creeping closer and closer to them. Not one person had been able to explain what had happened to them in the diner or why he had been assaulted as he had. There just was not the information that was needed.

Shaye turned from her front door. She had been standing there for the longest time, watching the night-time activity in her neighbourhood. She was afraid, she had finally admitted to herself, but grateful for the aid that seemed to be coming her way. Shaye just wasn't sure if it would be enough to protect her.

Chapter 8

Standing in his home office three days later, Slavin stared down at the mail that he had dropped to the desk top. A plain brown envelope, a larger one, was prominent on top of that pile. He stared harder at it before he closed his eyes, praying that it would have disappeared by the time his eyes opened again. That didn't work. The envelope was still there.

Reaching for his phone, Slavin simply sent a text to John, asking him to stop by at some point. He was beginning to get that mail that all of them had prayed would stay away. He turned then, heading for his bedroom to change from his dress clothes. Even though he worked primarily from home, he still dressed more formally during office hours. That helped to some degree to break his work life from his home life.

John paused as he studied his friend. He and Jerome had had a long talk about what Slavin and Shaye were facing. Neither could understand the whys of it or who. There just wasn't the information that they needed.

"Slavin?" John's voice broke into Slavin's thoughts. "Did you open it at all?"

Slavin shook his head. He had not reached out to open it. He had waited for John. He was afraid for his lady and that envelope wasn't helping to relieve that fear.

"No, I haven't. I don't know that I can." He looked up at his friend, their heights almost matching. "Who is doing this, John? Do we even have any idea?"

John shook his head. That was a question he kept asking himself, the question going unanswered. He stared around the office, liking the colour of a light jade as well as the dark wood floor. The cream trim suited the colours, reflecting from the dark oak flooring.

"No, we have no idea. We're working with what we have, Slavin, but there isn't a lot right now. Let's see what you were sent." John snapped on latex gloves before his head bowed. He prayed for whatever it was that Slavin was now facing.

The contents were dumped out on the desk top, causing both men to stare at them and then at each other. John's pen was out to move the objects around.

"This is strange, Slavin. I don't see any letter but this? A tiny cow, a picture of a farm, a little tractor. This is not making any sense." John looked around the room, searching for any answers that were not there for him to find.

"It is strange." Slavin frowned. "I don't know what to say, John. This would be more what Shaye would receive, given her line of work."

"It would be. Let me reach out to her." John walked away, his phone out as he called Shaye.

Shaye stared at her phone as John described what Slavin had just received. She shrugged.

—

"I have no idea what it would mean, John. I don't do assessment or estimates on farms, only houses. The maximum footage that I do is less than an acre. That's not enough to have whatever those objects stand for. I have never been on a farm. Not once. Not even in my personal life." Shaye finally set her phone down on the kitchen countertop, uncertainty in her movements. It was just too bizarre what Slavin had received.

Slavin tossed and turned for a good portion of that night, his mind too troubled to sleep. He rose at last in the early morning hours, reaching for his Bible and settling down in his prayer corner, his favourite armchair in his living room. He had no idea what he faced that day but he knew that he would track down Shaye at some point. Slavin had a soft smile on his face as he thought of that lady. She was interesting, in an interesting career, and could challenge him without putting him down. He didn't want to see her walk away from him, not ever.

Setting aside his troubles for the most part, Slavin moved through his day, not sure why he was feeling as he was but something was about to happen. John had been in touch, just asking that Slavin stay safe. He had snorted at that, hearing John's laugh for the other end of the phone call. He had asked how he did that when they had no idea who was after either Shaye or himself.

Shaye finally shoved the keyboard tray back under the desk but didn't rise. She studied the grandfather clock in the corner of her office, showing dark against the pale cream walls of that room. She was frustrated, she knew, not just by the adventure that she and Slavin seem to be mixed up in but also by the email that she had just read. Someone was fishing for information, she decided, and then rose, walking away from her office and to the outside of her house. Shaye paced her back yard, troubled in spirit and mind before she was heading for the front yard. Her steps stopped as she saw the man waiting for her before she stalked towards him.

"You just had to show up, didn't you?" Her words caused Slavin to turn from where he was studying the front of her house.

He grinned at her before he reached to hug her, standing with his hands on her arms when he released her.

"I did. We need to go out for a meal, Shaye. Would you join me?" Slavin waited patiently for Shave to decide. If she didn't go tonight, he planned to keep asking her until she did. At least, that's what he hoped to do. Nothing seemed certain any more. He was still unsettled by what he had found the night before.

"And if I say no?" Shaye studied him more closely, seeing the fatigue in his face but also the peace.

"I'll just keep asking. We've been linked somehow, Shaye. I don't know why. And it seems coincidental to us sharing a meal at that diner. I would like to know which one of us that they were following."

—

Shaye stopped her light movements to stare at Slavin and then across the road. Her neighbour waved at her as he headed into his house, a frown momentarily crossing his face. Slavin was right. They had been targeted or at least one of them had been.

"I would too, Slavin. I just don't know how we find that out." Shaye moved away from him, into her house to retrieve her purse and then locking up after herself. She took the hand that he had stretched out for her, not really knowing that she had.

"I don't know that we can. John is puzzled but is not setting it aside if he can help it. Peter reached out again. He would like to meet with us and discuss things from his point of view." Slavin laughed as Shaye just threw up her hands. "You don't think so?"

"I know that he will have plenty of suggestions. I just don't know how to live with those. I can't. John is already stepping in. Did you know that I had an off-duty officer around here all day?" Shaye's voice was tight with frustration and fear.

"I had the same. It's what our police do, Shaye. I'm part of that group just because I work with the detectives and the techs. You became part of it when we went through what we did." Slavin parked at a favourite restaurant, his eyes on her and not the building. "Is this okay?"

Shaye nodded, not thinking of where they were. She frowned at the window, not seeing the bright sun that was starting to set.

"How do we find out, Slavin? You need to go on with your life and so do I. We can't really until this is over. And don't tell me that it will take months. I can't do that." Shaye blinked rapidly, tears momentarily blinding her. "I have a life to live and so do you. I know that I'm repeating myself. It's what I do." She glared at him as he laughed before he was out of the car and around to help her out of the car. Shaye stared down at their linked hands, not even sure what he was saying with that but feeling cherished and protected both.

—

Chapter 9

Three days later, Shaye stopped her car and just sat, staring at the house in front of her. She could not enter the driveway, not yet. She felt the officer beside her twisting in his seat, his eyes narrowed as he studied the property.

"Shaye?" Timothy watched her, knowing that something had stopped her from driving up to the property.

"I can't go in there, Timothy, and I should. I just can't." Shaye pulled away from the driveway, heading towards the police station. "Can you tell me why?"

"Pull over, Shaye." Timothy was out of the car as she did so, almost running around it to shove her across the console and to where he had been sitting. He shoved the gears into drive and took off, his phone out to call for help. He too had a bad feeling about that place.

Shaye stared at him in shock, not sure what had just happened but something had triggered this. Her head twisted as she stared behind her, seeing the vehicle that was approaching this.

"Timothy?" Her voice quivered with fear.

"I know, Shaye. I know. Hang tight. I'll try and lose them. We have help on the way. I just don't know if it will come in time." Timothy's hands on the steering wheel were firm and tight as he twisted it to change lanes and then turn corners at a high speed. He knew that Shaye was praying, he could hear her. He could also see how tight a grip that she had on the seat belt and the door handle. "Good. We have company of the right kind." Timothy sped past the responding officers, seeing one spin around and follow them back to their department.

Timothy was out of the car, his hand on Shaye's door as he yanked it open and then pulled her from the vehicle, heading on a run for the back door which opened and closed quickly behind them.

John was waiting for them, a hand out to draw Shaye into his office. He shoved her down, a bottle of water handed to her before he was in the hallway just outside of his door. His eyes never left Shaye as he listened to Timothy.

"She couldn't drive in?" John was surprised at that for a moment.

"She just couldn't. I felt something off as we stopped, John. I just didn't know what. Shaye drove off and then I had her switch places with me. This is so strange. Who is doing this to her and why?" Timothy was puzzled by that. He was friends with Slavin from school and didn't think that either of the couple had done anything to merit this.

"We don't know at the moment, Timothy. That we're trying to determine and just can't at present." John studied him. "You're friends with Slavin. Do you have any idea if he has any enemies?"

Timothy shrugged, thinking through what he had been asked.

—

"I don't know of any. That's not to say that there isn't. We both know how this works, don't we?" Timothy was angry for a moment. "How do we do this, John? We need to protect both of them. I can't see us being able to do that all the time."

"And neither can I." John sighed as he continued to watch Shaye. "Shaye? What happened today?" He walked back into his office to perch on the corner of his desk. "Timothy tells me that you just couldn't drive into that property."

"No, I couldn't, John. It's like there was a huge gate in the way that was locked and I didn't have the key." Shaye studied him before she sighed. "It was God, wasn't it? He stopped me, didn't He?"

"He did, Shaye. He did. Now, what do we do with you? How do we keep you safe?" John was at a loss as to how to do just that.

"I don't know, John." Shaye was on her feet. "I need to go home and work. This was not the only estimation I was to do today. I need to access the information on the next one." She walked away, Timothy beside her as she headed for her vehicle.

Slavin rose from his desk, stretching and then rubbing at his forehead. He had been deep into research regarding a nearby town, the archives not really telling him much. He frowned at that. There should be information there and wasn't. Slavin sighed to himself. That meant a trip to that town soon and he really didn't want that. He didn't feel safe travelling and he didn't want to ask anyone to go with him, not wanting to put anyone at risk.

—

His phone in his hand, Slavin walked towards his kitchen, squinting at the clock. It was past supper time but he didn't have any appetite. Instead, he scrolled through his messages, pausing at the one from John. Slavin grew afraid for the lady who had appeared in his life, that she would disappear and he would never find her again.

"John? Slavin. What can you tell me?" Slavin reached for the mug of tea that he had poured, heading for his living room. He found his favourite chair as he listened to John.

"Your lady? Shaye? She was out on an estimation today and couldn't drive into the place. Timothy brought her here. We have no idea what had happened. He did say that they were followed." John was frustrated at the lack of information that would help solve whatever it was that Shaye and Slavin were involved in.

"That happened? There has to be a reason why she didn't drive in." Slavin frowned, trying to determine just what that meant. "She drove away?"

"She did and then Timothy took over. Our feeling is that if she had gone in, she would have at the very least disappeared. And we have no idea why." John turned as he heard a sound from Slavin. "Slavin?"

Slavin just shook his head. He had no words to say and he told John as much.

"How do we keep her safe, John? She's not going to want an officer with her for much longer." Slavin didn't admit that he and Shaye were talking on a regular basis, every night in fact. They had been out for a few meals but Shaye was reluctant to do that. Just why that was? She couldn't or wouldn't say.

"I know, Slavin. And that's when it becomes dangerous for her. We still don't have a good reading on what happened to you two. By now, we should. You have both provided the lists of family, friends, and acquaintances that we asked for. Nothing is obvious from there."

Chapter 10

Slavin's hand tightened on Shaye's the next afternoon as they walked towards a diner. She had agreed to meet him for a meal. Instead, he had driven by her house and offered her a ride, finding her frowning at him before she agreed. He had parked near a favourite restaurant, not liking that he felt watched.

Shaye's stepped slowed as she studied the men in front of her. She sighed to herself before she began to pray, begging for God's protection. They were there, not for their good, she just knew.

"Slavin? Those men? Do you know them?" Shaye's voice was barely a whisper.

"No, I don't. And I don't think that they're meaning us any good." He looked around before he was on the run, tugging her with him and heading away from the restaurant. He shot down an alleyway, hearing running footsteps behind them before he fell, the bat thrown at him entangling in his legs.

Shaye screamed as they fell, not able to protect themselves from that. She felt the men's hands on her, dragging her to her feet despite her frantic attempts to escape. She could hear Slavin's voice raised in anger and protest before they were both shoved away from that area and into a vehicle. Shaye felt her hand gripped by Slavin's, not daring to look at him. She knew that he had been hurt. She had heard the groan that had come from him.

Slavin tried to study the men and memorize as much as he could about them. That didn't seem to be happening. He began to pray earnestly, begging God for protection and release. He knew that God was there and was allowing what had happened to them. He just didn't like it or like the fact that his lady was once more in danger.

The couple had no idea where they were headed. The windows in the back of the van were just too dark for them to see out of. Slavin's hand tightened ever harder on Shaye's and found hers tightening on his. He was afraid, more afraid than he had ever been. They were in the hands of someone who meant them harm and that was scaring them both.

John turned from Slavin's door that night, frowning that the other man had not answered. They were to share a meal and a time of prayer but it didn't seem as if that would happen. He pulled out his phone to scroll through his messages, nodding to himself that he had been correct. There was no message from Slavin nor was there one from Shaye. He had come to expect one from both of the couple, just reaching out to see if their adventure was over.

Feeling a hand on his shoulder, John looked up, frowning at Peter as he stood beside him. How did Peter come to be there, John wondered.

"Peter?"

"I know, John. I'm here and I don't know why. God told me that I was needed here." He nodded towards the door. "Slavin's not home?"

"He was to be. We were to share a meal. I can't raise him on his phone either." John's face grew grim.

"Was he with Slavin? I've had word from the street that they were to disappear and do that today. It seems as if that has been correct." Peter paced the sidewalk, his mind racing as to what they could or should be doing. There were no clear answers that he could determine.

"That's what I am afraid of, Peter." John reached for Peter's arm, pulling him with him. "Come. Let's head to my home. I have to do some research and you can help. Where's your wife?"

"At home. She refused to come, stating that she would stay there and pray." Peter gave a grim smile. "We both know what happened. Let's find them and bring them home."

John rose for his computer an hour later, taking with thanks the mug of coffee shoved at him. Edward had appeared as well, determined to help in the search.

"Have we narrowed it down any, Peter?" John thought that they had but he was not sure.

"We have. I just don't know if that's where they will be. It's bizarre to say the least." Peter was not as familiar with Edward but watched that officer closely. He sighed. This is strange, Lord, he thought. They disappeared in broad daylight. Now, where would they be?"

"I reached out to our street sources." Edward looked up from his notes. "They haven't gotten back to me yet. Either they don't know or they are running scared."

"Likely both." John sighed, not likely what he had found. "I don't like what we're finding. I need to prove it and that I will." He reached for his phone as it chimed, frowning at the email that he had received before he smiled. "Emma Finlay is weighing in. I don't know how she knew but she does."

Peter gave a smile for a moment. Emma's husband, Abe, had a security team as well and Peter was well acquainted with that lady.

"She's good. She finds people and addresses and information that no one else seems to be able to find. Emma will track them down without a doubt." Peter yawned suddenly. "I need to get on the road, John. Let me know what else my team can do." He walked away, leaving John and Edward staring after him before they exchanged a look.

"How do we go on now, John? You're the investigator." Edward grinned at John.

"I am and right now, I'm the newbie on the team. I'll talk it all over with Jerome in the morning. He is aware that Slavin is missing. Our guess is that Shaye is with him. We can't find her." John locked the door after Edward, rubbing at his forehead as he walked back through his house. A headache was starting and that he really didn't need at the moment.

A soft chime from his phone had him reaching for it. A source on the street had reached out, not confirming where the couple was but that he had seen them taken. He would leave information for John with a local store. John knew the store and that the owner would be on the search for the couple as well.

Sitting on his bed as he retired, John stared at the dark hardwood flooring. He was troubled for his friends, not able to rest fully until he knew that they were safe. And just how safe they would be, he didn't know. He was suddenly and deeply afraid for them.

Chapter 11

The next morning found John heading for that very store, wandering through it and taking in the new merchandise that had appeared. It was a favourite store of his, stocking coffee, teas, and whatever was needed for them. His hand reached for a mug and he headed for the cash counter.

The store owner nodded as he bagged the mug, slipping in the letter that awaited John as well. He waved away John's money, sending him on his way, a prayer uttered for John and his investigations. That man was well aware that Slavin and Shaye had disappeared. Word was out on the street, and they were being searched for.

Once more back in his vehicle, John searched the area, not seeing anyone who stood out to him. And if he was being watched, he would have noticed that. He reached for the letter, reading it and then sighing. The person from the street who had left this information really hadn't helped much. Or had they? John was driving off as quickly as he could, heading for the department and his computer to search.

Sitting back from his desk an hour later, John looked up as Jerome appeared to sit in front of his desk.

"What do you have, John?" Jerome reached for the evidence bag, his eyes on the younger man before they dropped to read what he held. "You've verified this?"

"I have. It doesn't make a whole lot of sense. There are no buildings there. Nowhere that they could be hidden. Why leave us that address?" John was frustrated and his face showed it.

"How be you and I take a drive out there and have a look around?" Jerome was on his feet. "There must be a reason that this address was left. That was your next step?"

"It was. I was coming to find you but you found me first. We need to find Slavin and Shaye. This doesn't help close this case." John watched out of the side window of the car as Jerome headed that way.

Jerome parked a block from the address, both men searching for someone who stood out. But there was no one that they could see.

"What now, Jerome? We search?"

"We do, John. Let's head that way."

The two men walked that walk, pausing as they stopped in front of the address. It was what they had expected, an overgrown, weed-filled plot of land that didn't look promising at all for their case. They shared a look before they headed to search it, each taking a side and walking back and forth until they met in the middle.

"Nothing that I can see." John was more frustrated than before. "Why send us out here? Unless.." His voice dropped away as he turned to study the building. "That one, Jerome. That one that is so broken down. Could there be something there?"

"It's possible. Let's see if your hunch is right." Jerome walked rapidly that way, pausing in the doorway. He could feel the evil in the building and that disturbed him.

"Jerome? I don't like what I'm feeling." John paused as well before he reached to turn on the large flashlight that he had retrieved from the car. He shone it around, frowning as he did so.

"I don't either. Let's search and then get out of here."

The two men searched as rapidly as they could, John reaching for an envelope that had his name on it. He frowned at it before he was running from the building, Jerome behind him. Back in their vehicle, John stared at the letter and then at Jerome.

"Who is doing this, Jerome? I feel as if I am on a wild goose chase." John carefully opened the letter, hearing Jerome muttering that he agreed. His eyes scanned it before he was handing it to Jerome. "This is not making sense."

"No, it is making sense, John. They sent you here to the empty lot, knowing that you would find nothing and then would search further. This letter has what you need in it. It gives you a name but not an address. I recognize the name from years ago. He was big in town but had to leave due to failed investments and fraud. I don't know if we ever caught up with him." Jerome handed the letter back to John. "I think that you would have been too young to know. But Slavin's family had run-ins with this man. What he's facing could be part of a revenge plot."

John nodded. That had been his feeling, that someone was out for revenge against Slavin. It didn't explain Shaye though.

"How would Shaye be involved?"

"That we need to think through." Jerome parked his vehicle in the police lot, shifting on his seat to study John. "You're from this town. You've been out on the streets. What have you heard?"

John shook his head. He had heard nothing about this man or his doings. That much he was sure of.

"I don't know him or what he's been up to. I guess people aren't talking. They seem to be afraid to talk to us."

"And they will be, if this is who it is. He's known to be ruthless. I have heard rumours over the years about him." Jerome watched as John walked away, defeat in his demeanour for the moment. Jerome could only pray for the young detective and then for the couple. He feared for their very lives if they were in this man's hands. But they didn't have confirmation that they were.

John looked around later that night, hearing a sound at his back door. He crept silently that way, the lights off in the kitchen, before he yanked open the door and reached for the person standing there. He stood in shock as his hand tightened on the arm of the person who he held.

"Shaye? What? Where did you come from?" John shifted her to a chair before he was outside searching, a hand out to lift Slavin to his feet and then into the house. He had not expected to find either one at his home. John frowned at them before he shut and locked the door, reaching to turn on only a low light before he turned to them. "Where did you two come from?"

Chapter 12

Slavin stared up at John, frowning at him. He had no idea that he had found John. His attention then turned to Shaye before he was on his feet, gathering her to him and then turning for the living room. Slavin sank down onto the couch, Shaye held tightly in his arms. His eyes closed as he struggled to breathe and then to try and make sense of what had happened. He lost that battle, his head going down on Shaye's as he slept.

Shaye had not moved once Slavin had gathered her to him. She too slept, leaving John to stand and stare at them in consternation. They would need to talk but for now, the couple needed to sleep.

John reached for his shoes and then a large flashlight, heading outside to search. He found no evidence of how the couple had appeared. It was just too dark to do that. He would search in the morning.

Returning to the indoors, John stood in the living room, his eyes on the couple before he reached for his phone.

"Jerome? It's John." John could hear Jerome setting down a mug.

"John? It's late." Jerome knew that John would not have contacted him unless it was necessary. "What's going on?"

"It's strange, Jerome. Slavin and Shaye just showed up at my house. I can't track where they came from at this time of night. They look very much to worse for wear." John paced his hallway, his eyes tracking to the couple every time he passed that doorway.

"They did?" Jerome sat upright, his mind whirling with possibilities. "Listen. I'll send a patrol to sit outside tonight. Keep them there. I'll be over."

Jerome reached for his jacket and then his shoes. His wife was away that night, at a ladies' conference with the church, and he was glad of that. He reached for his phone once more, calling in a physician who worked with the department on cases like this. The couple needed to be assessed, at least quickly, before too much time went by.

Standing in John's kitchen, Jerome listened as the physician spoke quietly with Slavin. That man had awakened and had reluctantly stood and laid Shaye on the couch. Slavin was not moving from her, that much was obvious.

"Has he said anything at all?" Jerome waited patiently for John to speak.

John shook his head. Slavin had only roused when the physician spoke with him. Shaye was just not rousing at all.

"Not yet. He's been out of it as has Shaye. I don't see that they're harmed to a great degree but we need to wait for Silas to finish."

Silas turned at last, tucking away his stethoscope and then rising to walk towards John's and Jerome.

"What can you tell us, Silas?" John finally spoke, his eyes on the physician."

"They have been abused to a certain degree, John. I would think as well, just from their condition, that they had limited food and water. I have drawn blood and will drop it off at the lab. Talk to me tomorrow afternoon. If you need me to return, just call me." Silas walked away, shaking his head before praying for the couple. He had no idea what they were involved in, but it didn't seem that it was for their health or their good.

John approached Slavin, finding that man watching him. He sighed. This is where he needed to speak with Slavin and Shaye both but he didn't know how much information that they would get.

"Slavin? What happened?" John heard Jerome's footsteps as he too found a seat nearby.

"I don't know, John. I really don't know. I can't remember anything for the last few days. And Shaye has said the same. I want whoever this is. And I want to know why." Slavin's head went back on the chair as he slept.

John nodded, sharing a look with Jerome. It was about what they had expected, but not what they wanted.

"I'm off then, John. Call me if they do say anything. We need to find out where they were for the past few days and who had them. I'm just not sure that we'll do that." Jerome walked away, a puzzled look on his face. He had no idea what had happened to the couple and from what he could see, he didn't think that

---

they could be able to say much. That bothered him to no end. All he could do was pray for them.

John was on his feet in the early morning hours, hearing soft sounds moving around his home. He stood and watched Shaye, finding her spinning in the hallway. She froze as she saw him before she walked towards him.

"John? Where are they?" Shaye had a frightened look on her face that John didn't like.

"The men? Who had you captive, Shaye?" His hand on her arm turned her gently towards the kitchen where he pulled out a chair and made her sit. His eyes were assessing her, not liking what he was seeing.

"Them. They said that we couldn't leave. That we had to work for them. Only, I don't know why. Do you?" Shaye's words were almost tumbling over each other, not how she usually spoke. Fear was driving that in her.

"No, I'm sorry, Shaye. I don't know that." John set a mug of coffee in front of her. "You haven't eaten for a while, have you?"

Shaye stared at him, wondering how he knew that before she shook her head.

"They wouldn't let us. They made Slavin and I just sit in chairs for the whole time, only letting us up briefly. Where is Slavin?" She twisted on her chair, trying to find the man who had tried to protect her.

"He's sleeping, Shaye. In the living room. I need you to talk with me, and tell me what happened." John reached for a pad of paper and pen, knowing that

Shaye may well not remember much more than Slavin had.

69

Late that night, Slavin paced inside his own home. He had finally walked away from John, Shaye's hand tight in his. They had needed to leave even though John had not wanted them to. He had found his car and then driven Shaye to her home, walking through it before he had hugged her and walked away. That was something that Slavin had not wanted to do but knew that he had to. They both needed time and space to come to grips with what they had gone through.

Sighing, Slavin finally sat at his desk, pulling up his word processing program on his computer and then making his notes. He frowned. There just didn't seem to be a valid reason for them to be taken. His work was such that he didn't feel threatened by anyone. Now, Shaye's work was different and he feared for his lady as he had become to think of her. How did she stay safe? His head finally bent as he prayed, begging God to protect Shaye and help them to solve whatever it was that they were involved in. He wanted to go on with his life, and he wanted Shaye to be part of that for the rest of their lives.

Shaye had rested her forehead against her front door after Slavin had walked away, her hand on the lock. She didn't want him to leave her, not ever. That was not how she was as a person. She was very independent and had always maintained that she didn't need a man in her life. Slavin was changing her thoughts. Her heart raised in prayer for her friend, knowing that somehow they were still in danger.

Turning to head for her kitchen, Shaye's feet slowed and then she stopped. She was more than a little worried about her work. Going into places to do estimations had never bothered her, not until now. The scare that she had experienced just recently had changed that. She no longer felt safe doing what she loved and that angered her. Shaye wanted whoever it was to be brought to justice and that done yesterday.

Her hand found the leaves of her plants in the kitchen as she pulled off the dead ones and then disposed of them. Her hands were busy with routine work even as her mind raced with the possibilities of what had happened to them. John had not been able to explain what was happening or even tell her that he knew who it was. There just wasn't the information that was needed.

Shaye reached for a bottle of juice, her hand resting for a moment against the closed refrigerator door before she was pacing towards her office. She pulled up her emails, sorting through what was there. Sitting back at last, she stared at the email that had just popped up. It was to her personal email and she didn't know that person. How did they find that? Shaye simply forwarded the email and its threat on to John and Jerome, knowing that she would have to answer their phone calls at some point. She just didn't want to do that.

John paused as he stared down at the paperwork on his office desk. He was on call overnight and had just returned from a crime scene. The older man had been murdered and there was little evidence to say who had done that. He frowned. The name had come up with Slavin and that worried John. He turned as he heard footsteps, finding Jerome there.

"John? What can you tell me?" Jerome found a seat in front of the desk, watching as John sank wearily into his own chair.

"Not a lot at present. He was murdered. The thing of it is? His name came up with this to do about Slavin. Slavin's related to him, I think somehow. And I don't know why this would happen." John sighed. "He was well liked in the community. He had no enemies that I can determine as of yet."

"Someone wanted him dead. And we will determine who and why." Jerome bowed his head as he prayed for his young detective.

"That's what's puzzling, Jerome. How would you go about finding that out?" John was willing and eager to learn, knowing that Jerome had years of experience in just this that he needed to draw from.

"That's a good question, John. So far, you're doing what I would do. Have you reached out to Trackers, by chance? Emma there and her team can find information that no one else can. They've been a great help over the years." Jerome watched John carefully,

"I have. She's been in touch. She has been away with her husband's security team, just back today. Emma has started what she can and thought she'd have some information for us by tomorrow. This is not making any sense, you know that."

Jerome gave a brief smile. It was not making any sense, that he had to agree with.

"Talk to Slavin and Shaye over and over. They'll get tired of that. Shaye, I suspect, will tell you off. That's fear and uncertainty coming through when they do that. Talk to their family and friends. Sean has been around, trying to connect with you. That hasn't happened."

"No, it hasn't. We've ended up playing phone tag. I'll reach out again today." John sighed, feeling the weight of the investigation on him. "And we have those other investigations too. How come so many all of a sudden?"

"There has been an increase. And we have discussed that as leadership here. Do what you can during your shift. Take the time away that you need to. If you don't, you'll burn out and quit on us. You're too good of an officer to have that happen." Jerome was on his feet, walking away, leaving John staring after him.

Edward approached John as he was leaving that day, just walking out with him. He was puzzled by what had transpired with the couple.

"What's going on with Slavin and Shaye? Do we even know?" Edward wasn't prying. He was just asking in general, knowing that John couldn't say.

"We don't as yet, Edward. Have you talked with Slavin at all? I know that you're friends." John stared at the keys he held in his hand.

———

"No, I haven't. He's been avoiding me and that's not him. Something is going on and I would like to know what." Edward's head raised as he heard a voice calling his name. His hand reached for John, tugging him towards the gate from the police lot. "There's Slavin. He's looking for you."

Slavin watched as Edward and John walked rapidly towards him, a letter held in his hand. He was afraid and not much made him that afraid. Someone was threatening Shaye and he had no idea how to protect her. That lady just wouldn't let him. In fact, she had told him off and told him to go home. He hadn't seen the longing in her eyes as she watched him do just that. Shaye needed him in her life. She was just too afraid for him.

Chapter 14

"Slavin? What's this?" John reached to take the letter from his friend, a frown on his face. "When did you get it?"

"Just about thirty minutes ago. I was at Shaye's and that was on my windshield. She doesn't want me around her. I don't get it. We have a connection that I can't walk away from." Slavin paced, not seeing the men watching him from across the rose.

"You do have a connection. She's telling you to stay away because she's afraid for you. She does want you there. I've seen the way that she watches you." John opened the letter carefully, his gloved hands handling it with care. He frowned at the wording. "This is very vague, Slavin. Just warning you that you're being watched."

"I know. They are out there. I feel them everywhere I go, including right now. How do we find them and stop this?" John paced in short, rapid steps, his agitation evident.

John prayed for his friend, knowing that he had no words to tell him that it was over or how to stay safe. It never worked out as they planned. They all acknowledged that God was in control and was protecting them. Nothing happened to them without God allowing it. He said as much to Slavin, drawing Slavin back to him.

"I know that, John." Slavin blew out a breath. "I'm sorry. I didn't mean it that way. I'm not angry at you. I'm angry at whoever this is. And I know that I have to let God have my anger. It's hard to give up, you know." Slavin gave a brief smile as John and Edward laughed at him before Edward frowned.

Edward was across the street, motioning for officers to go with him. The two men watching Slavin were quickly taken into custody, John watching as that happened.

"There were two men here, Slavin. Edward's just arrested them."

"They were that close?" Slavin paled at that. "And they're around Shaye's as well?" He was running for his car, not hearing John calling after him to wait. Driving away rapidly, Slavin headed for Shaye, out of his vehicle and at her door, pounding at it.

Shaye sighed as she heard the knocks or hammering at her door. She crept that way, peeking out to see Slavin there. Why was he back, she wondered.

"Didn't you just leave?" Shaye stepped back as Slavin moved towards her, the door closing behind him before he had her wrapped into a hug. "Slavin?" Shaye shoved at him, just not able to release herself.

"You're okay. I was so worried. Edward arrested men outside of the police department. I thought that you had disappeared again." Slavin stood back from her, his hands resting on her upper arms. "How do we do this, Shaye? How do we keep you safe?"

—

Shaye finally shoved away from Slavin to step backwards. That was her fear. That something happened to the man who she was beginning to care for. Slavin was working her way into his heart just as she was into his.

Neither couple had spoken about what had happened to them lately and they needed to. They were afraid to, the words driven at them driving their time in captivity deep within them.

Slavin sighed, his eyes on his lady.

"Shaye? We need to talk and talk about what happened."

"I know that we do. I just don't want to." Shaye blinked back tears, finding herself wrapped into Slavin's arms. "I have a friend who has reached out to me. He wants to meet with us. His name is Roane. Can we meet with him?"

"We can. I also have a friend who would like that. His name is Nickol." Slavin grinned at her suddenly. "Our friends have unusual names, just as we do."

"We do." Shaye worried her bottom lip. "Roane is a private investigator who I've used in the past."

"Nickol is a forestry officer. I've been involved in some of his investigations. When would they like to meet with us? Nickol has suggested on Saturday." Slavin waited for Shaye to decide, not wanting to push her too hard.

"That works. That's what Roane has suggested." Shaye suddenly hugged Slavin, just realizing that he

—

77

still held her. "Can we solve this, Slavin? I don't want anyone hurt."

"Someone has already been hurt, love, and that's you. And yes me." Slavin just stood, his chin on the top of Shaye's head, liking how she fit into his arms. "And we will solve it. John and Peter will both be willing to meet with us, if you want."

"That works." Shaye looked up at him. "These are all men. Don't you know any ladies who faced this?"

Slavin nodded. He did know of some ladies and he would reach out to them.

"I do, love. That I do. Let me see what I can set up for Saturday with some of them. Sean and Annie will want to be here."

"And you are worried about your nephew. I would be too." Shaye stepped away from Slavin, heading for the kitchen. "Since you're here, you may as well stay for a meal. It's just salads, if that's okay."

"That's more than okay. What can I do to help?" Slavin followed her, liking the colours and style of her kitchen.

Later that evening, Slavin set aside his phone. He had reached out to a former forensics psychologist, Darci by name, who had readily agreed to meet with them on Saturday along with her husband, their town's ETF lead lieutenant. They had faced life and death from a rogue police chief. More importantly, Darci was working on a profile for them of who was after

<hr>

them. Slavin knew that she would be spot on with what she said.

John turned from his living room window that same night, deep in thought before he began to pray for his friends, begging God to cover them with His hand and protect them. It was becoming harder and harder to know how they could do that in their humanness. And that worried him. He didn't want to see either Slavin or Shaye hurt worse than they had been or even killed. John was well aware that they had not told everything about this last time that they had disappeared and he needed them to do just that.

—

Chapter 15

Shaye was on her feet and at Slavin's home early on the Saturday morning. She had not slept the night before, spending it in prayer. She thought back over what the two of them had faced, knowing that they had not discussed it at all and should have. This tall handsome man was just taking more and more of her thoughts and she appreciated his protectiveness. Shaye was praying daily for her guy as she termed him and felt God's presence with her and with him. She just didn't know if that would be enough to protect them. That was her daily and hourly cry, for God's protection on them and for a swift resolution to whatever it was.

Slavin watched Shaye as she worked in his kitchen, setting out the squares and cookies that she had prepared. He turned to lift the roast pan from the oven, the roast of beef cooked and ready to be sliced. Between the two of them, they had prepared enough food they hoped to feed the number of persons who would be there. The group just seemed to be growing by person and person. Shaye wasn't sure about that but Slavin had simply wrapped her into his arms and kissed her, surprising them both. She had stared at him, a question in her eyes, reading his feelings for her in his.

"Who all is coming now, Slavin?" Shaye stood for a moment, a plate of cookies in her hands.

"John. Peter. Roane. Nickol. Doug and Darci. Abe and Emma who are friends of Doug's. Actually,

Abe is Doug's cousin. He has a security team and she has a business where she finds information. She has been working on this for us. A team member of Abe's wife has a family tree program that she has been working on and will send what she can release to us. And then there's Richard and Raleigh, another security team lead. We'll eat, spend time and prayer, and then look at what we have. We will solve this, sweetheart." Slavin eyed her as she thought through his words and then nodded.

"We will. I just pray that no one is hurt or killed before we do that." Shaye was sober as she spoke, her head raising as she heard a tap at the front door and then the door opening. John and Peter appeared, reaching to hug her and then greet Slavin.

An hour later, Slavin stood back from the living room where he could watch the group gathered. He nodded. Darci, Emma, and Raleigh had just moved in on Shaye. She was opening up to them, he decided, and liked the lady who was appearing.

Nickol stood beside his friend, his eyes on the group. He realized that he in fact did know Roane and was not surprised to find him there. He searched the others, who were in law enforcement, and nodded some more. Just maybe, he thought, they could move the investigation ahead and solve this before Slavin or Shaye were hurt any more than they had been. Skylor could see the interest between the two, finding them watching the other when they didn't think that they were being observed. He was glad for his life-long friend. Shaye seemed to be just who Slavin needed in his life.

—

"What are you thinking, Slavin?" Roane waited patiently for his friend to speak.

"I'm really not sure, Roane. It is just strange. This last time? We were taken, held in some decrepit house, abused and then let go. Somehow we made our way to John's house." Slavin was still puzzled by all that. I just don't see why or who."

"That is a puzzle, Slavin. And I don't know if we have enough information to solve it today. How do we keep you and your lady safe? That's the question." Roane shared a look with Doug who had stopped on Slavin's other side.

"That is a good question, Roane." Doug was nodding. "We've shared what we went through. Richard had shared about his team. Abe has shared about their team. Sometimes, God uses us to bring someone to justice here on earth. That has been what happened with us all." Doug was sober as he spoke, remembering just how close it had been for himself and Darci.

"I get that, Doug. I just don't have to like it." Slavin reached to hug Shaye as she moved into his space. He could feel the tremors shaking her body. "Okay, sweetheart?"

"No, I'm not. I don't know if I ever will be." Shaye burrowed against Slavin, hiding her face for the moment. "I don't like this, Slavin. We need to end this and find whoever is responsible. I don't know that we can without someone being killed."

"That is a good concern, Shaye." Doug spoke up. "And we will all do our best to prevent that. I have spoken at length with John and he has spoken with other officers who have faced what you are facing. It's tough to go through this. But know that God is here. He is walking every step beside you. Nothing reaches you that is not in His will for you. We don't have to like what happens but God is at work. He shelters you and protects you in ways that you may never know here on earth." He walked away at that, heading for Peter.

"He's right, sweetheart. Doug is right. Now, what have you discovered?" Slavin studied what he could of her face.

"What have I discovered? That I am terrified. I am on my own with no family around. I don't have that support and I need it." Shaye was sober as she looked up at the tall handsome man who had her wrapped in his arms.

"I know, sweetheart. Let me be your family. My family wants that. Annie has been hesitant to approach you to ask you for lunch, knowing how you would likely feel. It's okay to be afraid and want the comfort of your own family." Slavin tightened his hold on her. "Marry me, Shaye. Let me be your family." He didn't look at her but he felt the sudden stiffening of her body as she took in his words.

"Do you mean that, Slavin? We don't know each other enough to marry." Shaye stared up at him, not sure that she had heard him correctly.

"I do, sweetheart. I do. Pray about it. I don't want you to rush into a decision. For now, let's listen to what this group can determine and then we'll search it out more." Slavin turned her to face the group,

—

finding a seat for her and then sitting himself down at her feet.

Abe was watching him closely, assessing him. He frowned before he shared a look and then a nod with Richard. They had decided something, he thought, but they weren't ready to share with anyone at the time.

Locking up as the group left, Slavin's hand rested against the steel door he had just locked. His head dropped as he thought through the day, a smile creeping across his face as he thought of how Shaye had reacted to each one and had been driven to find out as much information as she could. It was who she was, he knew. Now that they had information, Slavin and Shaye would work through it with their friends here, knowing that the friends from other towns were just a phone call or email message away.

Chapter 16

Sunday found Slavin standing inside the church, looking for Shaye. She was to be there that day but still had not shown up. His phone was out as he searched his messages, not seeing one from her. He was running from the building, heading for his car, and then heading for Shaye's home. He was out of the car and at her front door, finding her just sitting on her front porch.

"Shaye?" Slavin was beside her, an arm around her, not sure what had happened. "Shaye? Talk to me. What happened?"

Shaye looked up, surprised to see him there before she was frowning at him.

"Slavin? What are you doing here?" Shaye straightened up, reaching to turn his wrist to see his watch. "We're supposed to be in church, aren't we?" She yawned, sinking back against his arm. "I'm just too tired this morning."

"You're not sleeping." Slavin frowned at her. "What did you get last night?"

"What did I get? I'm not sure what you mean." She looked up as she heard another set of footsteps. "John? What are you doing here? I didn't call you."

"No, you didn't but you need me here. As Slavin asked, what did you get?" John waited patiently for Shaye to respond.

Shaye finally pointed a finger towards the garage.

"In there. A box or parcel or whatever you want to call it. I didn't open it. I shut down, I think, and just collapsed here." She yawned again, her head going down on Slavin's shoulder before she just fell asleep.

The two men stared at her and then at one another before John was on his feet and heading for the garage. Slavin watched him walk away before his arm was around his lady and he just cradled her to him.

John's footsteps paused as he approached the garage, reaching to open the side door and stepping inside. He saw the package right away and walked that way, stopping to stare down at it. It had Shaye's name on it in bold black lettering. He sighed. This was starting now, he thought, and reached for his phone to make the call to the crime lab.

An hour later, he stepped back as the senior tech approached him, a frown on his face.

"What do you have, Stu?"

"It's strange, John. Dead flowers. Dead bugs. And a map of her property. I'll send you the photos but I just don't understand it." Stu was puzzled by what was in the package. "And we searched the box. Nothing stands out that doesn't seem to be part of the box."

"That is strange, Stu. Send me the photos then and I'll talk to Shaye. Slavin's not leaving her side." John turned to watch the couple as they stood nearby.

"He's found his lady. I'm glad. I know Shaye from church. She's a wonderful, caring, compassionate lady who takes care of others before herself. Slavin's the same way. They suit one another."

John walked slowly towards the couple, his eyes on Shaye. He could see the apprehension in her eyes as to what she would be told but also the fear and determination to solve whatever it was.

"John? What did you find?" Shaye's voice was steady and confident, not as it had been earlier.

"What did I find? Interesting material. Dead flowers. Dead bugs. And a map of your property." John watched her carefully, seeing her frown. "You're not planning on selling it, are you?"

"Absolutely not. Do you have photos that you can share?" Shaye reached for his phone, studying the photos. "This is strange, John. I don't like mums, which is what they are. Bugs don't bother me. And this map. It looks like my property but it's not. The coordinates are wrong."

"They are? How do we find out where it is?" John was puzzled, sharing a look with Slavin.

"Come on inside. We're not making church today. I can pull up a program to find that property. Slavin? You two will want to eat. I have sandwich stuff that you can use." Shaye walked away, not seeing the grin on John's face or the open smile on Slavin's.

"I guess that I got told, didn't I?" Slavin ran after her, an arm around her to draw her close to him.

Thirty minutes laters, John stood, his sandwich in his hand as he watched Shaye search for the property.

"Here you go, John. It's not even in this town. What does that mean?" Shaye looked up at him, frowning.

"Can you send me that link?" John handed over a business card with his email address, knowing that something had just changed in their investigation. "I'll look into it. But for now, what can I do for you two?"

Slavin shrugged. He had no idea what John could do other than to solve the investigation that day and that was not happening, that much was clear. His eyes were on Shaye as she studied John and then studied him.

John walked away an hour later, not quite happy with what had been discovered. Stu had been in touch, just to confirm what Shaye had discovered. They now had the task of tracking down the owner and that seemed to be buried in numbered companies. John sighed before his phone was out and he was sending the link to Emma, asking for her help.

Slavin reached to hug his lady, holding on just a little bit longer. He was greatly worried about her and that showed in how he held her.

"Slavin? You were to have lunch with Sean and Annie, weren't you?" Shaye was worried that he had missed time with his family.

"It's okay, Shaye. He understands. Listen, Mom and Dad are back from vacation tomorrow. I would like to take you to meet them, if you will." He watched her closely, seeing the hesitation on her face. "It's okay. They know what's been happening and are not afraid. I don't think whoever this is will go after my family. It's not how it seems. And besides, Dad was in law enforcement until he retired as was Mom. They know how to take care of themselves and us." He grinned as she frowned up at him.

"I guess. When?" Shaye reached for her daytimer calendar, pulling up that week. "I don't have a lot on this week, but that can change. Sometimes I get calls to do urgent estimation." She frowned at her calendar before she looked up at him. "I don't think that's such a good idea, is it?"

"Not likely. For now, ask Emma to look into any names. She offered that as they were leaving. If she can't, then she has staff who will." Slavin hugged her, dropped a kiss on her forehead, and then walked away, hearing the lock click into place behind him.

Chapter 17

The following Monday, Slavin shoved back from his desk, a frown on his face. He paced his office before he was pacing through his house. The research into his town's archives was disturbing to say the least. He had been approached by a member of the historical society to search through their archives. Something was off, he was simply told, and that he had found to be correct.

Slavin stood and stared at his computer monitor. Records were being changed from what they had to been to something different and he needed to determine who and why. He sighed to himself. That meant a trip to that very building that housed the historical society and he wasn't really ready to do that. Slavin simply had no choice. He rose once more from his desk and headed for his back yard, to walk the perimeter of it, watchful for anything that seemed out of order.

The chiming of his phone had him reaching for it, squinting at it in the bright daylight. John was looking for him. Just where was he, that officer had questioned. Slavin sent a quick reply before heading around his house, to find John and Peter both standing there, grim looks on their faces.

"John? Peter? What brings you here?" Slavin stood in front of them, a hand rubbing at his face. He could hear the sounds of nature in his ears, wishing to be elsewhere instead of standing on his front walk, confronting a police officer and a security team member.

"Inside, Slavin, and now." John shoved at him, turning him to walk back around the house and inside.

Slavin spun as he stopped in his kitchen, not seeing the touches of colour that his mother had placed. His frown deepened.

"Just what was that about?" Slavin refused to back down from the two.

"We've had word that someone wants you dead. Do you know why?" John stood almost toe to toe with Slavin, a worried look in his eyes and a stern and grim look on his face. He knew that Peter was searching outside for anything that didn't belong.

"Dead?" Slavin swallowed hard. "Who? And why?"

"We don't know that, Slavin. Word just reached us from the streets that a contract had gone out on you. We need to go over your investigations as much as we can." John waved a search warrant at him. "This is for you." He almost slapped it at Slavin who grabbed for it.

Slavin stared at him and then down at the folded piece of paper that he held. He sighed to himself.

"Do you have any idea what you're looking for?" He watched John closely.

"No, I don't. Jerome sent me to go over what you're working on. It has to be something recent. At least, that's what we're being told. And Peter has been asked to ensure that your security is as tight as it can be. If needed, we bring in his team or another security team." John paced the kitchen, his eyes on Slavin.

"The investigation that I'm involved in right now is for the historical society. I was approached to delve into the archives." Slavin rubbed at his cheek once more. "The online records are changing day by day and that shouldn't be happening. That means that someone in that building or society is doing that."

"Show me." John's hand on Slavin's shoulder turned him that way. "But first, Slavin, let's pray. I worry about you and yes about Shaye." John didn't state that Shaye had reached out to him already that day, anger sparking from her voice as she stated that she was forwarding threatening emails to him. Just what was he going to do about them?

Slavin nodded, knowing that God had to lead them and that was a fact he was confident in.

"Okay. So, I've been working on this for the past couple of weeks inbetween other research. Every day I go in, something has changed. Someone is trying to change the history of the town. We may need to look into finding someone who can research that better than I can. I don't do ethical hacking."

John was nodding, having already reached that conclusion.

"So, we'll find someone. What else?" He waited patiently for the other man to speak.

"What else?" Slavin shifted on his chair, his eyes searching his office. Nothing seemed off but he felt watched every time he was in there. His security feed had not shown anything wrong. "Something's off in here, John. I think you and Peter need to search in here."

John was on his feet, his hand out to draw Slavin from the room before he was calling for Peter. The two men began a systematic search of the office, not liking what they were finding. Someone had accessed the office, likely when Slavin was home and outside with the doors unlocked. It wouldn't have taken that long to place the cameras that they found.

Slavin stared at the equipment that John had placed in evidence bags and then dropped on the kitchen table before he was away to search the rest of the house. Peter had been around the outside and not found anything there. That told those two men that whoever it was? They were interested in what Slavin was finding.

"When?" Slavin drew in a deep breath. "When I was doing yard work? I leave the back door unlocked when I do. When I'm at the back of the yard, I don't watch the house. I haven't felt that I needed to." He sighed, a deep deep sigh of frustration and fear. "I guess for now, the door is locked unless I am right outside of it."

"That's likely a good idea." Peter turned from where he had been studying the back door. "I don't see that someone broke in. For now, let's take a look at your security system. We can upgrade it if necessary, but I think that you have a good one." Peter was as good as his word, turning back from it to study the other man.

"I see. Peter? I think that you and I need to meet and meet with Shaye as well. It's time to make some plans, isn't it?"

Peter was nodding as he spoke.

"It is, Slavin. When can we meet?" He turned as he heard the front doorbell.

Slavin paced that way, opening the door to find Shaye just launching herself at him. He could see and feel the fear, no terror, that she was feeling. He simply wrapped her into his arms and held on tight, prayers whispering for the lady who he had acknowledged that he loved.

Chapter 18

Shocked at how Shaye was reacting, Slavin simply wrapped her into his arms and moved backwards as both John and Peter ran for the outdoors, the front door shut behind them. He studied his lady before he was into the living room, seated on the couch and wrapping her tight into his arms. He could feel the shuddering that wracked her body but couldn't get her to respond to him at all.

John was back into the house, his eyes on the couple before he shook his head. He stood for a moment before he found a seat, not looking away from Shaye. Shaye on the other hand refused to look up, too terrified to do anything other than cling to Slavin whom she felt was her lifeline at the moment.

Peter had taken off to search around Shaye's home, surprised to find the door still wide open. He frowned as he called for officers to go through the house, not sure at all what he would find if he went in. Peter was not prepared to be accused of tampering with any evidence. None of the officers or even Peter had been prepared to see the destruction in her home. She wouldn't be living there for a while, they all decided, looking around at what had been destroyed, including the large holes in the drywall in every room. Someone had meant harm to Shaye. They just didn't know who.

Slavin shared a look with John before his eyes closed and he began to pray for his lady. John picked up the prayer before he was on his feet, heading for the kitchen and returning with a bottle of water that he tucked into one of Shaye's hands. She looked briefly at him, causing him to draw in his breath before he found his seat again.

"Shaye? Sweetheart? What happened?" Slavin waited patiently for her to respond, feeling her shifting against him before she finally looked up, reaching to push the hair from her face.

"Someone broke into my home. I was on the back deck and heard it. I just ran." Shaye sniffed, trying to control her emotions. "I didn't even have my keys so I couldn't take my car." Her head went down against him once more. "I am so afraid, Slavin. Who is doing this and why?"

At her words, John was on his feet, heading for his car. He drove off, finding Peter waiting for him on the city sidewalk. John nodded at him before he was into the house, shocked at the destruction. He spoke with the officers before he found Shaye's purse and walked away, studying the people gathered on the street. He didn't know who were her neighbours or who were strangers. A though occurred to him and he returned to speak with one of the patrol officers, who nodded, his phone out to take photos of the crowd.

"Send those to me, Sam. And I mean as soon as possible." John looked around. "Let me know when you're finished. For now, Shaye is with Slavin and will stay there." John headed back towards Slavin's home, finding that man standing on the front porch, searching for anyone who meant his lady harm.

"John?" Slavin didn't say or ask anything more. He saw the shuttered look on John's face and grew even more afraid for Shaye.

"Her home's destroyed, Slavin. It will need a lot of work for her to be able to go home." John hesitated as he saw Shaye in the doorway. "Shaye? Thank you for running. I've been in your home."

"How bad?" Her voice was barely a whisper.

"Really bad, Shaye. We'll need to find a place for you to stay for now. It will be a while before you can go home." John smiled with sympathy as her face crumpled and then she turned and walked away.

"John? What aren't you saying?" Slavin stood beside him, his eyes on his lady.

"Her home is destroyed to some degree, Slavin. Whoever it was? They were angry that she wasn't there for them to take. And we still have no idea who or why." John walked away at last, heading for another crime scene, his heart troubled for his friends.

Slavin searched for Shaye, finding her curled up in a chair in his office. She had found that room, knowing that Slavin would be there soon and at work. Sitting at his desk, Slavin studied his lady, unsure as to what to say or how to act. This was a situation that he had never faced before.

"Slavin? Who is doing this? Do we even know?" Shaye's voice was still tear-filled.

"I don't know that we have that information yet, sweetheart." Slavin studied his computer monitor, knowing that he had work to do, but his lady needed him. "What are your thoughts?"

"That someone hates me enough to try and destroy me. It may be a competitor. Our field can be ruthless at times. Some of the estimators don't care who they hurt as they try and get the biggest contracts that are out there. I don't care. I just want to help people and this is my way of doing it." Shaye's eyes closed as she sought comfort from her Heavenly Father.

Slavin had nodded and then his attention went to his emails and then to the search that he was conducting. He knew that he would need to head for the historical society and determine just how bad the situation had become. He had no idea why someone would be tampering with the online archives. Slavin had seen this somewhat in the past, a disgruntled employee responsible for the damage. This time, it was not obvious what was happening but he was determined to find that person or persons responsible.

Shaye's eyes watched Slavin as he worked away, a sigh drawn from her. She needed to discuss something with him, but that wasn't happening at the moment or so she thought. She looked down for a moment, not seeing when Slavin looked at her. Shaye jumped as she felt an arm around her and then Slavin's voice praying for her. She was beginning to look for him wherever she went and longing for his company when he was away from her. Shaye was falling in love with this tall handsome man, didn't know what to think or do, and didn't think that she had anyone that she could speak with.

Slavin simply hugged his lady. He was in love with her, he knew, and wanted nothing to happen to her. He was well aware that she had been terrified that morning and that she still had to walk back through her house. She also needed for find a place to stay and that troubled him.

Sean hesitated for a moment as he saw the couple before he found Slavin's desk chair and sat, his eyes not moving from his brother.

"Slavin? I heard what happened. Annie has asked if Shaye would come and stay with us, at least for tonight." Sean's voice was quiet, not revealing the troubled thoughts.

"You would do that?" Shaye looked up at him, a frown on her face. "I have nowhere else to go. I need to go home."

"And you will, Shaye. That's a promise. We will get you there to go through the house. John will call us. Peter is still around as is his team. They'll watch out for you." Slavin knew without a doubt that was what Peter would do.

"He would? But what about you? Who protects you?"

Chapter 19

Walking towards her home, Shaye realized just how far that she had run that day, seeking protection and comfort from Slavin. She shook for a moment as John stopped in front of her, not wanting to walk into her home but knowing that she had to. Her insurance agent was inside at the moment, walking through with Edward before he spoke with her.

"Shaye?" John once more awaited patiently for Shaye to respond, a slight smile on his face as she refused to look at him. "It's okay, Shaye. We have officers here still to protect you. We'll walk you through. Your insurance agent has been here for a while, documenting everything. He does with to speak with you." John bit at his lip for a moment, sharing a look with Slavin who shrugged.

"I see. Is it that bad?" Shaye didn't know what to ask or even what to expect in an answer.

"Unfortunately, it is, Shaye. You'll not be staying here for a few days. Your work? You'll need to pack up what you require. Unfortunately, your computer was smashed." John winced as her eyes closed. "One of Peter's men have reached out to a friend and obtained a new one for you. They'll set it up for you at Slavin's, I would think. Somehow, we need to keep you two together as much as we can."

Slavin was nodding, knowing that was exactly what he wanted. It would depend on what Shaye wanted, though. This was her life and she had to be the one choosing what she did and where she went.

"I guess. I'll need to find accommodations, won't I?" Shaye blew out a breath. This was not how her day was to have gone. She prayed, begging God to turn back time to the day before and let her live today over again. Only that would never happen. She knew that.

"We'll find you something. For tonight, you are with Sean and Annie. And yes, I will be there." Slavin didn't say anything more, catching the brief look of relief and thanks that crossed his lady's face.

"That's okay, Slavin. But you have work to do." Shaye walked away from him, leaving Slavin to drop his head before he ran to catch up with her.

"I'm not letting you walk through this alone, sweetheart. If I did and something happened to you, I don't know if I could live with that." Slavin just reached for her hand again, an audible prayer just for her whispered, begging God to protect his lady. He didn't realize that he had put it out there.

His prayer caused Shaye to look up at him, marvelling once more at his height. She frowned as she listened to his words, realizing that he had indeed claimed her as his lady. That fact gave her hope that God had heard her prayers over the years for someone just for her.

Hesitating at the front door, Shaye was reluctant to step through into the entryway. She saw the damage to the door and grew even more afraid. Who had done this and why? Those were questions that no one could answer for her. Shaye's head was bowed for a moment as she prayed for strength and courage to move forward, choosing life instead of defeat.

Her free hand covering her mouth, Shaye stood in her living room, her feet just not able to carry her forward any further. Her head twisted as she took in the damage, not just to the walls and floor from the heavy sledge hammer and thrown paint, but also the destruction to her trinkets and belongings. Her heart failed her as she looked around, feeling Slavin's arm around her as he hugged her close to him.

Slavin waited patiently for Shaye to move as did the insurance agent and John. None of them had seen this kind of damage in a home before. They were all troubled for the lady standing in their midst. John began to pray, the other men picking up when he stopped, before he looked at Shaye.

"Let's walk you through your house, Shaye. Then, you'll need to pack what you can and take it with you. We'll find you a place to say." John watched with compassion as Shaye finally nodded and then moved through her home, tears on her cheek that he didn't think she knew that she was weeping.

Shaye finally stood in her office, her eyes on her desk and then her filing cabinet. Her computer was destroyed but her files were stored to a cloud program. She turned suddenly to find herself just wrapped into Slavin's arms, his care and compassion for her coming through loud and clear.

"Let's pack you up, sweetheart, and then see where you want to be." Slavin nodded at John,

Edward, Sean and Annie as they moved through the room. Peter and his team were there as well, reaching to help.

Annie drew Shaye away at last towards her bedroom.

"What do you need to pack up in here, Shaye? Let me help you. The guys have plenty of boxes. Do what you can today. We can come back tomorrow." Annie watched the lady who had her brother-in-law's heart. That was obvious by how he was treating her and looking out for her.

Shaye finally nodded, moving to the dresser as Annie moved towards her closet. Shaye frowned for a moment. This shouldn't be happening, she thought. Who hates me this much? She just didn't understand how or why God had allowed this to happen. Shaye would be spending time in prayer just to try and understand.

Annie suddenly just reached to hug the other lady, knowing that she needed that contact. Shaye clung to her for a moment before she stepped back, taking the warm cloth that Slavin was handing her to swipe at her face.

"I just don't understand, Annie. Who does this? I mean, this is my life that has been damaged and destroyed." Shaye reached for a novel that had been torn in two. "Someone was very angry to do this."

"They were. I am so glad that you had sense enough to run and to run to Slavin. He'll do what he can to protect you, Shaye. That's a given." Annie turned back to folding clothes and placing them carefully into a box. She saw Sean watching from the hallway before he moved on. "We have friends who will move in to help you clean out and get rid of the garbage. It's not what should have happened but it did. Then, we work on what is going on with you two."

Shaye stared at her for a moment, feeling the bonds that had bound her heart for so many years loosening. She didn't have friends in that town, no matter how much she wanted that. She was reserved and people took that as meaning that she didn't want anything to do with them.

"You mean that, Annie? I don't have friends here. I have led a very solitary life." Shaye sighed once more, her eyes on the shattered pictures on the floor.

"We do mean that, Shaye. Slavin is not letting you walk away. He is reacting and treating you differently from any other lady who he knows. That shows us that you are special to him." Annie turned back to face Shaye. "And we don't want to lose you as a friend."

Chapter 20

Late that afternoon, Slavin turned and searched for Shaye, not finding her in the living room of his home. He walked through the house and then was outside, walking around it. Shaye just was not there. His phone was out as he sent a text message to her, a frown on his face as she responded that she was with Nickol and Roane. Where was he? Slavin simply shook his head, locked up his house and headed for Roane's home.

Watching as his friend walked towards him, Roane sighed. He had been investigating as he could among his other cases and didn't like who or what he was finding. That was a given, he decided.

"Slavin? What have you gotten mixed up in?" Roane asked that half in jest.

Slavin shrugged, not quite sure what to answer.

"What have you found that we hadn't? And I know that you have." Slavin paused in the doorway. "Shaye's here?"

"She is. So are Sean and Annie and your nephew. I hear that your parents are almost home."

"They are. I miss them and just need them at this point." Slavin was sober as he spoke, knowing that his words were true. It didn't seem to matter how old you were. When you were troubled or sick or whatever, you just needed your parents.

"You need them, for sure. In with you now. We're in the office. And it is a mess for now." Roane detoured through to his spacious kitchen, reaching for the tray that he had been preparing when Slavin appeared.

Slavin stood for a moment, his eyes on the activity before he was sitting beside Shaye, causing that lady to jump. Shaye's eyes were huge for a moment before they narrowed as she glared at Slavin, who just grinned back at her.

"You didn't know that we had left?"

Slavin shook his head, his eyes studying the lady beside him. He didn't want any harm or any more harm to come to her. He just didn't know how to prevent that.

"I didn't. I was deep into research." Slavin bit at his lip for a moment before he looked around, finding the others studying him carefully. "I think I know why. The historical society. Someone has been changing the online information."

"And that is cause for concern." Roane frowned at him even as he heard Nickol speak. "What did you just say, Nickol?"

"I said that we've been investigating someone who is linked to the historical society." He mentioned a name, seeing consternation on the other's faces. "We need to find out what we can and then approach John. And Peter did say that he was bringing in friends."

"He is. A lady named Emma. Her husband is friends with Peter and has a security team." Roane looked down at the sheaf of papers that he held. "And Emma finds information and people that no one else can."

"I've met her." Shaye didn't look up to see the surprised looks on the faces of those around her. "She was involved in a case that I had a few years ago." She looked up at that point. "And it did involved someone here in town." She said the name, knowing that information was out there. "And just how does she relate to what we're going through now?"

"That's what we're working on, Shaye. Her name came up late last night when I was speaking with a friend." Nickol didn't look around. "He's another investigator from a newby town. We'll connect you two with him at some point." He looked up a frown on his face. "I still don't see how you two have connected other than going to the same church and living in the same town."

"That's what we don't understand, Nickol. We don't have mutual friends. Or we didn't until now." Slavin tightened his arm around Shaye, causing that lady to frown at him.

"I don't see any connection either." Shaye shoved away from Slavin to pace, disappearing for a moment to find room to do just that.

Annie was on her feet, following her, her young son running for the lady he had claimed. She gave a small smile as she saw Shaye reach to pick up Andrew before she was hugged tightly and smothered in kisses, a smile on her face as the young boy did just that. Annie walked towards the door as she heard a tap at it, opening to find John and Edward both there, grins on their faces as they stepped inside and closed and locked the door behind them.

"You two are here? You're supposed to be off duty." Annie continued to frown at them.

"We are, Annie. We're here as just friend today, to see what we can do for Slavin and Shaye." John peeked into the living room. "Although I see Andrew seems to have it well in hand." Andrew was just refusing to be put down, his arms tightening around Shaye's neck if she tried that.

Shaye looked around, laughter on her face for a moment, as she finally was able to hand Andrew off to his mother despite that young man's protests.

"He certainly does. But what are you two up to?" Shaye moved away and back to the office before they could respond.

"Did she just do that?" Edward stared after her, not sure what had happened.

"She did, Edward. She's pacing and trying to come to terms with what has happened and who we suspect. She is also trying to come up with a way to end this today." Annie simply shook her head at the two men before pointing towards the office. "They're all in there." She watched the two officers head that way, hearing the greetings called to them, before she bent her head and began to pray for her beloved brother-in-law. Sean's arms came around her as he too prayed for his brother, not sure where the investigation was headed or even how much more danger the couple

were in. And that Slavin and Shaye were in danger?
That was not far from anyone's mind or prayers.

Chapter 21

Standing in the office of the historical board director, Slavin felt afraid and didn't understand why. He had had contact with this man before and never had that feeling. Today, he was ready to turn and run, not stopping until he was somewhere safe. The director had stepped away for a moment, unbeknownst to Slavin standing and watching him, hatred on his face.

Slavin turned at last, walking from the office, not seeing the man's secretary at her desk. And she should have been. That fact caused him to increase the speed of his steps as he headed for the outside and then his car. Slavin stood for a moment, his keys in his hand as he looked back towards that building. Something evil was in that building, a feeling that he had never had before. And he wanted to know why and who.

The director stood inside the building, near the exit doors, watching Slavin. His eyes narrowed as he thought through Slavin's questions before he nodded. Slavin was on to something and that something involved him. He would need to take steps to stop the younger man from finishing off his investigation. The director had no idea who had asked Slavin to undertake that but he would find out. And that person would pay in a way that they would wish that they had never asked for an investigation. At this point, the director really didn't care if anyone lived or died.

Slavin drove away, keeping an eye on his rear view mirror. He was afraid still and growing deeper afraid. Someone in that society was up to no good and into crime. He just wasn't sure which one.

Pulling into a parking lot at a local diner, Slavin sat for a moment before he reached for his phone. Reaching only Roane's voice mail, he left a message, simply requesting that Roane contact him. He had an investigation that he felt Roane needed to do for him. Scrolling through his messages, he smiled at the ones from his family and then stopped at the one from Shaye. His smile grew more tender as he pondered the character of that lady and knew that he didn't want her to walk away from him ever. Slavin's eyes raised as he stared out of the windshield, not seeing what was in front of him. Instead, he saw Shaye as she had been yesterday, determined to solve their mystery, standing up to his brother and the two officers, and then her tenderness with his wee nephew. Slavin wanted Shaye to stay forever in his life. He had finally acknowledged that he loved her, even with how short a time that they had been acquainted. He had never believed in love at first sight. Shaye had changed that for him.

Even as he contemplated how to date Shaye, Slavin had to acknowledge his fear for himself and his lady and the family. He could only trust God to protect them and guide them as they walked through the journey called Life. He was choosing life to its fullness. Slavin refused to let whoever it was draw him into and drown him in the waters of despair and fear. That was not how God had called him to live his life.

The chiming and vibration of his phone drew his attention to the screen. A soft smile covered his face as he read Shaye's response to his question of whether he could take her out for a meal. The positive response and happy face emoji caused Slavin to grin. Yes, he thought. She was not averse to spending time with him, even though they were both dangerous to others. He sent a quick response, just asking if he could pick her up at that time to go for that meal. Slavin grinned at the question marks that responded to his own question before a simple yes came through in a new text message.

Shaye had stared at Slavin's message before a soft smile lit her face. She was dangerous to know, she had to acknowledge to herself, but Slavin was not walking away. He was keeping his word. She turned as she heard a soft tap at her door and walked that way, peeking out to see Slavin standing there, his back to the door as he studied the area, on guard for anything that seemed to threaten her. Opening the door, Shaye had not been surprised to be caught into his arms and hugged. The kiss had been what had surprised her. She too was falling in love with this tall handsome man holding her. All Shaye could do was pray for God to protect them both.

That night, Slavin finally set his phone to one side. Roane had finally been able to reach out to him, simply asking who he wanted him to investigate. Slavin had been surprised when Roane had stated that he was not surprised that Slavin needed this board investigated. There had been word on the streets for months that something was off about one or two members. No one was sure which ones though. That was kept far too hidden.

Slavin paced his home that night, not ready to sleep even though he was exhausted. The text messages were starting, growing increasingly vile and evil with each one. He had forwarded them on to John, who had asked if he was safe for the night and to not go outside, no matter how much he wanted to do just that. Patrol vehicles passed his house every hour, passing Shaye's as well. The thoughts were that if whoever it was couldn't get to Slavin and draw him out, that they would try to abduct Shaye once more and use her against Slavin. There never was an answer to why she had been unable to enter that property.

Shaye turned from her work three days later. It was a Friday, early afternoon, and she felt that she just could not do any more work that day. Not sleeping at night was not helping. Shaye reached for her phone and then stuffing her bank card and driver's license into her phone case. She needed to get away but just didn't know where to go. That frustrated her. Shaye was restless without knowing why.

Heading for a nearby park, Shaye found her favourite bench, setting down the bottle of water beside her. Her eyes closed as she sought refuge with God, praying for safety, comfort, peace, and hope in what she was facing. She had not spoken with Slavin since their meal days ago. He had been reaching out and then stopped. Shaye didn't know if it was because she wasn't answering or if it was because he didn't care or if it was because he was missing. She was sure that if he was missing, someone would have been around to speak with her. Even with her eyes closed, she sensed a presence beside her, feeling the bench move as someone sat there. She sighed to herself. She wanted to be on her own and that wasn't happening.

Shaye refused to look up or at the person. She sensed that whoever it was didn't mean her harm. A few minutes later, the bench moved slightly again as that person stood. She heard the soft footsteps as someone walked away. Her eyes opened as she gazed around. Whoever it was no longer was around her. Shaye stared at the envelope lying on the bench before she reached for it, seeing her name neatly printed on it. She frowned before she stuck it into the pocket with her phone and then was on her feet, moving back towards her home. She didn't see the men who stood where she had just sat, desperate to find her and frustrated that she was no longer there.

Chapter 22

Shaye stared at the envelope that she had placed carefully on her desk, not wanting to open it, afraid of what she would read. Her prayer was desperate as she begged God for answers to whatever it was and then for peace in the situation. She was choosing life, she decided, not death or defeat. That would not happen unless God willed that she go home. Shaye continued to pray for Slavin, his family, and their friends. She knew that his parents had returned and wanted to meet her. Shaye was just not sure that she wanted to meet them. She was uncertain as to where she stood with Slavin. He was watching her in a way that she remembered his father watching his mother, love in his eyes, but she just didn't think that she was reading him correctly.

Sighing as she heard the doorbell, Shaye walked that way, standing back far enough so that she was not seen. She frowned. She didn't recognize the couple who stood there. Then, Slavin and John appeared in her line of sight. Of course, they had to show up, didn't they? She returned to the kitchen, reaching for the letter and sticking it into her pocket before she walked back to open the door, to stand and stare at the four who stood there.

Slavin gave a grim smile before he wrapped her into a hug and then moved her back into the house enough so that the door would close. He had watched the vehicle sitting across the street from her home and had called John. John had appeared, assessed the situation and then called for patrol to come and arrest the men. The two men had fought with the officers, determined not to be arrested but their fight was short lived as they were handcuffed and then removed, their vehicle on a tow truck to take to the impound yard.

John watched Shaye closely. She has received something, he thought, and isn't ready to share with me. That's okay. I'm here as a friend and not the investigator today.

"Shaye? Are you okay?" Slavin waited patiently for her to speak.

"I am. Just what are you doing here? You're supposed to be working. And John is too." She frowned harder as the two men smiled.

"Not today. I'm off today, Shaye." John reached to hug her as he moved past her to the kitchen, intent on making their coffee. "And these are friends of ours. Abe and Emma Finlay. They wanted to meet with you. Emma has information that she need to go over with you two."

Shaye looked past Slavin at the couple, seeing their smiles but also seeing that Abe's smile didn't quite make it to his eyes. She sighed. What now, Lord? How much longer is this to go on? I've had enough already, Shaye thought.

"Hi. May we call you Shaye?" Emma simply reached to hug Shaye before Abe did the same, surprising that lady.

"You can. But I don't understand why you're here. I mean, I know what you do. I just don't know what you would have for me." Shaye stood for a moment, Slavin's arm around her before she moved away, heading for John to question him. "John? What's going on? I saw that car across the street."

"That car? There were two men inside very intent on watching your home, Shaye. Did you not see it earlier?" John was positive that she had and had just ignored it.

"I did. I didn't see anyone in it. I went for a walk and then came home. I was only gone for thirty minutes or so. What aren't you telling me?" Shaye was refusing to back down from him.

John shook his head. He didn't know if Shaye was that careless, didn't care, or even was aware of how much danger she still seemed to be in.

"I know how much danger I'm in, John. That hasn't changed. If anything, it has increased. I was watching around myself and walked away from the park. And yes, two men were there watching me when I did so. They were the men in the car." Shaye was standing toe-to-toe with him.

Abe, Emma, and Slavin watched, almost a look of amusement on their faces before Slain was beside Shaye, wrapping her in his arms.

"Don't shoot the messenger, sweetheart. He's only looking out for you." Slavin shook his head at John.

"I know. I just don't have to like it." Shaye looked around Slavin at Abe and Emma. "Now, what do you have for me?"

Emma grinned at her as she held up an envelope.

"This contains what we have found and proven. Let us go over it with you." Emma reached an arm around Slavin. "Where can we work?"

"The office." Shaye headed that way, Emma keeping step with her. The three men looked at one another before shaking their heads and following them.

Three hours later, Shaye locked her door behind the four, worn out from the information that she had been given. She set it to one side for the night, reaching instead for her pocket and the envelope. That was set down on her desk as she stared at it before turning and walking away, the lights to the office shut off. Shaye would deal with that on the next day, unless Slavin was as good as his word and occupied her day with a trip to the downtown area. That he had threatened as he left, a grin on his face daring her to say no.

Slavin was troubled as he sought his rest. Emma had provided so much information, he thought, almost too much to take in. And he knew that Shaye felt the same. He re-read the paperwork before setting it to one side. He needed to walk away from it for a while. Slavin grinned as he remembered the look on his lady's face when he asked her to spend the day with him. He wasn't sure if she would but he had every intention of trying to persuade her in the morning.

He reached for his Bible, needing to find the promises of God for safety, protection, and peace. Slavin wanted to live life with his chosen lady. He just didn't know if that would happen. All he could do at present was pray for her and then leave her in God's hands.

John studied the paperwork once more, a frown on his face. Emma was good, he knew, providing what she could and what she provided had been proven. He still needed to go over it with Jerome and that would happen on Monday. He reached to lock the paperwork away, not willing to leave it out. John turned to the living room window, standing in the dark as he studied the stars. He felt small that night, amazed at God's creation that was so vast but small enough that God had created for all of them to enjoy. He could only pray for his two friends, realizing that they were nowhere near close enough to solve the mystery.

Chapter 23

The next morning found Slavin staring at Shaye's front door. It was broken down and barely hanging by a hinge. He couldn't step into the house, that much he knew. Instead, he backed away and reached for his phone, calling in for help.

The officers moved quickly through the house and searched the outside. Shaye was not there and they could not tell how long it had been since she had been. Jerome frowned at Slavin for a moment before he moved into the scene and into the house, walking through it. It wasn't destroyed this time, other than for the door. And there were no signs of any struggle which he had expected fully to see. It was as if Shaye had not been home when the assault on her door happened or if she had been, she had managed to escape.

Slavin looked up as Jerome stopped beside him, to lean against Slavin's car. He turned to face the house, not looking at Slavin, knowing that man had questions and wanted answers, answers that he could not give.

"She's not there?" Slavin's voice was barely audible and tear-filled.

Jerome didn't think that Slavin was aware of how he sounded. He frowned for a moment, a thought crossing his mind. He watched as the officers moved to walk to Shaye's neighbours, to question them on when they had last seen Shaye and if they had heard anything over night.

"She's not, Slavin. I'm sorry. There is just no evidence of what happened." Jerome shot a glance at the man beside him. "Did she plan on leaving home this morning for any reason?"

Slavin had to shrug. He had no idea if she had. That lady had not told him.

"I don't know. I had come by. We had tentative plans to be together today." Slavin drew in a deep breath, frowning for a moment. "Her car's there?"

"It is. So if she left, she was either walking or someone picked her up. Would she have had a friend do that?" Jerome was grasping as the proverbial straw, he knew.

Slavin shrugged. He didn't know her friends, didn't know if she had planned on meeting anyone. Hearing a soft sound beside him, Slavin turned, finding Shaye near him. He simply reached to hug that lady, a nod to Roane and Nickol who stood beside them as well.

"Shaye?" Jerome stared at her before he turned back to stare at the house. "When did you leave?"

"Roane came by about six, I think it was. He had some information for me on a property that I had been asked to estimate the buildings on. He wanted to drive by it early before anyone would be up and around. Nickol joined us." Shaye stared in horror at her home. "What happened?

"What happened? Someone broke down your door and walked through your home. We couldn't find you and had no idea where you were." Jerome was almost angry, not at Shaye but at whoever it was.

"I can see the door is broken. Now, I have to find someone to fix it." Shaye was angry at once more having to repair something in her home. "Will they just stop destroying my home? What are they trying to prove?"

Jerome stared at her for a moment, taken aback at her words.

"Why would you phrase it that way, Shaye?" He waited somewhat impatiently for her to gather her thoughts and speak.

"They're costing me money, Jerome, and my insurance company money. Are they trying to have that company drop me as a client? Or are they sending a message that I'm not understanding?" Shaye didn't see the startled look that was thrown her way.

"Shaye?" Jerome waited for her to look at him. "Why would you say that? That your company might drop you?"

"Isn't that what they do when the claims grow to be too high? Drop you and then you can't get insurance. And if I can't get insurance, then I can't work. I have to have business insurance in order to go onto the properties." Shaye stared at Jerome as he gave a choked sound. "Jerome?"

"What you just said, Shaye? About business insurance? If you had to shut down and couldn't work, who would take over?"

Slavin's arms tightened on his lady as she shook in fear for a moment. All he could do was pray for her and claim God's promises of protection and safety.

"A competitor. We're really a close group here, Jerome." Shaye turned to him. "You know, none of you have asked for that list of estimators. And why not? I'm sure that you have a list of archivists."

"We have been remiss, Shaye. We should have. Our thoughts, I think, were that Slavin was the target. It may be you as well or just you and Slavin is incidental to it all. Please provide me or John with that list today." Jerome walked away as Shaye protested.

"He needs it, sweetheart." Slavin shared a look with Roane and Nickol. "We should have asked as well but our focus was elsewhere."

"And I think that you'll find that was done deliberately, Slavin." Roane rubbed at his cheek. "I had that thought and have found the list. I have been looking into them. I passed that list on to Emma this morning."

Shaye turned her head to watch him before she nodded. This was what Roane did. He thought outside of the box as the saying went. Now, maybe something would happen to solve this and both Slavin and she could get on with their lives. Only she didn't want to get on with her life if it didn't include Slavin.

Slavin nodded. This was what he had expected as well. His eyes dropped to the lady still standing in the circle of his arms. This was not how their day was to have been but it was how God had allowed it to be.

Chapter 24

Standing in the entryway to her home hours later, Shaye listened to Slavin on his phone. He had had a call come in that he just couldn't avoid, much to his distress. He wanted to spend the time with Shaye, helping her to understand what was happening and just couldn't.

Shaye walked away at last, heading for her office. She was not surprised to see Roane and Nickol there as well as Peter. His team was around outside, that much she was aware of and had protested at. Peter had just grinned at her and said that they had all wanted to be there, that she needed them. His grin had widened as she had just snorted at that and then walked away. He didn't see the small smile on her face, a smile that grew for a moment as she thought through the men now in her life. She had never had that many before and those who were married? Their wives were reaching out to her. Shaye had agreed to a Bible study on Monday night, knowing that she would as safe as she could be.

Slavin pocketed his phone, a thoughtful look on his face. That had been Abe who had called, just checking in on the couple. Emma had a pile of information for them, he stated, and would the couple be around on the next day? They were planning on heading their way with the information. Slavin had agreed that he would be. He just didn't know what Shaye had planned. He needed to stop that lady in her pacing and running away in order to have a conversation with her. And that didn't seem to be happening any time soon.

Locking up after the group, Shaye paused for a moment, her hand still on the lock. A soft smile crossed her face as she pictured Slavin, reluctant to leave her but knowing that he had to. A kiss had been dropped on her cheek and her hand now found that spot. Shaye had no idea where they were going as a couple. She only knew that she didn't want him to walk away from her. He made her feel safe, adored, and cherished.

Walking back through her home, Shaye paused in the office, her eyes on the neat piles of paper that sat on the credenza near the windows. She sighed. She had had enough of this for the night. Reaching to close the curtains and then to turn off the lights, Shaye hesitated before she shut the decorative glass door behind her. She needed that barrier to this investigation that night. She was tired, worn out, discouraged, and whatever other emotion that she could not name flowed through her. She reached instead for her Bible, needing that time with her Abba Father to get her head back on straight as she termed it.

Slavin paused in his bedroom, his hands stopped as they were reaching to pull his blankets back. A thought had come to him and he almost ran to the office to jot it down. He stared at the paper and the name before shaking his head. It couldn't be that easy, he decided, not at all. He would pass it on to John but also Emma. A soft chime from his phone had him hunting for it. Slavin read the text message from

Emma and shook his head. He had no idea how she did it but she had pinpointed the name and simply asked that he stay as safe as he could. Emma was afraid for Slavin and his lady.

Peter sat in John's office that following Monday. He had been approached the day before by a youth on the street, handed a grubby piece of paper, and then watched the youth run from him. He had been disturbed, to say the least, as he read the note.

"Peter? Who gave you this?" John looked up once more, studying the man who was his cousin and a close friend, even though there was a slight age gap between them. Jerome sat beside Peter, watching John closely to see how he would conduct the investigation. He had no doubt that John was on the right track.

"A youth from the street." Peter refused to name the youth, wanting to protect him as much as he could. And if that youth was correct with the name, he would be at great risk of injury or even death.

"Okay, so how did he come up with that?" John shared a look with Jerome. "And Emma has sent information that I need to go over with Jerome and then with Slavin and Shaye."

Peter was on his feet, frowning at John for a moment before his face cleared.

"They'll have that information and likely more that Emma has released to them. She never sends you anything that she has not verified and that will help move the investigation forward. She will release more to the individuals involved, with the caveat that they not give it to the investigators. Emma feels that is her prerogative."

"And it is. Emma is the one investigating it. If one of her employees is the one who finds and verifies the information, that person is the one who speaks with the investigator. It is just how she has set up her office." Jerome had had a few conversations with Emma over the years.

"It is and it is true that is how it has to be. Things can be lost to translation or misunderstanding if that doesn't happen." Peter walked away, knowing that he had to be at his training site but not wanting to be there. He wanted to protect the couple but they were refusing any and all offers.

Shaye turned from the homeowner of the property that she had just been through. The man was a member of their church but she didn't feel safe. Shaye walked rapidly away from the house, turning as she sat in her car before driving away. Reaching out to John, Shaye simply asked if he had ever investigated that man. She had a bad feeling about him.

John stared at her text message, frowning at it. Robert Clark had been on their radar for years, rumours rife about him, but there had been no solid evidence linking him to any crime. That seemed about to change. He sighed as he reached out to an investigator that he knew, that did financial investigations. Barnabas would be back to him when he had information. John sat for a moment before he was asking Shaye to send on any addressed that she was asked to estimate to Barnabas' son, Samuel, a title searcher. Just maybe, he prayed, that would be how they ended this for Slavin and Shaye and let them lead the life that they seemed heading towards.

Slavin stared at Shaye that evening. He had arrived, a meal in hand, just wanting to spend time with his lady. He had not expected her to name the man that she had.

"You're serious?" Slavin reached to hug her, finding her hugging him back. He simply prayed for his lady, feeling her relax against him.

"I am. I was there today, Slavin, but it seemed as if it was a set up. He's not selling. I don't go in and estimate for mortgage renewals. And that would not have been what he was after." Shaye's head rested against Slavin's shoulder, "I think that he was fishing for information."

"He may well have been. You talked to John?" Slavin had no doubt that she had. His hand rubbed along her back, the light yellow sweater that she wore soft under his hand.

"I sent him a text. And then I reached out to Emma." Shaye sighed, knowing that she had to continue. "He has asked if I would send any addresses where I have been asked to estimate property to a friend of his."

"Samuel. He's a title searcher. He and his wife, Aideen, had an adventure that almost killed one of them. We need to head to Elmton and talk to that group." A grin lit up his face. "In fact, two detectives, the police chief, and the minister of their church all had life and death adventures as they called it as well as a security team and another group of friends that are close to Samuel."

Shaye pushed back to look up at him, shock on her face.

"What did you just say?" At his nod, Shaye's head went down against him. "So, what you're saying is that we are not alone in this?"

"Never alone. There are many in the area who had had this happen to them. And they would all be willing to speak with us. I know that without even asking them. It's what they do." Slavin's arms tightened on his lady.

"And I am going to owe so much to everyone. I don't think that I can afford this any more." Shaye grew sober, knowing that she didn't have the funds to pay.

"It's okay, sweetheart. No one ever expects you to pay. It's how they reach out to friends and they all consider you a friend of theirs. One of them describes it well. He calls it being the hands and feet for God on earth." Slavin felt her nod and then felt her relax even more before he was seating her and setting out their meal.

Chapter 25

A week had gone by since Shaye had almost run from Robert Clark. She had found him watching her at church before his attention went to Slavin. She had also found evidence that someone had been around her home, not leaving anything, not trying to break in, just walkking around it. Her security feed had picked that up. John had been around, taking a thumb drive with that evidence. The man's face was not clear enough to identify him. All he could do was warn Shaye to be careful.

That afternoon, Slavin's hand reached for Shaye's as he helped her from his car. They had run away that day, heading for Elmton and the group of friends there. Barnabas had reached out to Shaye, just to pick her brain as he termed it, gathering what information that he could. Samuel had also been in touch, just asking for any addresses that he could do a title search on. And that had happened. There had been a couple that Shaye had refused to do the estimation on, simply sending those people to someone else. They had protested but Shaye had refused to back down.

Slavin's work had increased dramatically and he was at a loss to understand why. Some of the investigations that he had been asked to undertake made no sense. He had sat back from his desk that very morning, a thought crossing his mind that these were an attempt to draw him away from his investigation into the historical society. Shaye had been vocal when he mentioned that, confirming his thoughts.

Walking through the downtown of their hometown, Slavin studied the people around him. He was being followed, of that he was certain. John and Peter had emphasized that to him, warning him to watch for anyone meaning him harm. They had stared at him when he asked how he would know that, when the only people he saw were people from the town.

He hesitated at a shop before he was into it and then his purchase tucked gently into an inside pocket of his jacket. He was meeting Shaye for lunch or so he thought until a text message had come through. Shaye was sorry but she couldn't make it. Slavin frowned at that. That was not Shaye to do that. Running for his car, Slavin headed for Shaye's home, pulling to a stop in front of it and was then out and running for the front door.

Shaye stepped back from the door, watching as Slavin entered her home and then shut the door. She was puzzled at his appearance.

"Weren't we to meet down town at the diner?" Shaye felt the tightness of Slavin's hug and the fear that he felt.

"We were. I got a text message from you that you wouldn't make it. It didn't sound like you." Slavin kept an arm around his lady as he searched for the text message. It had disappeared. "That's strange. The message is gone but it stated that you couldn't make it and that you were sorry."

"I never sent that. I was looking forward to lunch with you." Shaye blew out a deep breath as she heard footsteps on her front porch. "Now who?" She peeked out of the door and then backed away from it. "I don't know that man out there. Do you?"

Slavin moved to where he could see the porch, his head shaking as he did so.

"No, I don't but he seems to think that we'll let him in." Slavin's arm around Shaye drew her back further from the door. "Wait. John's out there and seems to know him."

"He is? He does?" Shaye waited somewhat impatiently for John to greet the man, a hand out to shake the other man's hand. "Do we let them in or not?"

Slavin gave a low laugh. His lady was being very cautious. His phone was out as he received a text, tilting his phone to show Shaye. She snorted at the message from John, just asking if they would let them in, causing Slavin to laugh harder as he reached for the door.

John studied the couple, and they were a couple in his mind whether they had cameo to that conclusion themselves or not.

"Shaye? Slavin? Aren't you two working?" John frowned at them for a moment before he sighed. "What did you receive?"

"A message from Shaye's business phone stating that she wasn't able to make our lunch date. And before you ask, that message has disappeared." Slavin

<hr>

stared at John before his attention went to the man beside him. "Care to introduce us?"

"This is Frankie Brennan from Riverville. He's the lead detective. Emma asked him to bring material for us all." John watched Shaye carefully, a frown on his face. Something was going on with her and he wanted to know what. Knowing Shaye, however, he knew it would take a lot of talk and discussion to get her to state what that problem was.

"You two were correct in not opening the door." Frankie grinned at them for a moment. "And Emma has sent information for you. If you like, we can go over it. Some of what you're facing seems to tie in with my town."

"It does? And how would that be?" Shaye walked away from the men, heading for her kitchen. "It's lunch time, did you know that, John? All I can offer is sandwiches and some fruit. I wasn't planning on eating at home today."

Slavin grinned as he followed her. She was becoming feisty, he decided, a result of her frustration and fear. He hugged her, a kiss delivered to her cheek, before he was helping her. His grin widened as she commented that he shouldn't have kissed her. What were they doing, dating or something? Slavin looked around, not seeing John or Frankie for a moment before he kissed her again and said that yes, they were dating. Had she forgotten?

John dropped his folders to the tabletop before he was reaching for the fridge for water for them all. It would be a long afternoon, he thought, and they really did need to speak with the couple. Only he was no longer sure how they would take what had been discovered.

"Shaye? Slavin?" Frankie sat back at last, reaching for the folders that he had dropped to the floor beside his chair. "We've eaten. You've been gracious that way, Shaye, and thank you. We've spent time in prayer. What we need to do now is go over what we can with you."

Shaye shifted her chair closer to Slavin, finding his arm around her. She was deeply afraid all of a sudden and that fear was driving her to shut down. Only Slavin was not letting that happen this time. Her head turned as she studied him, finding him watching her.

Chapter 26

Her hand resting on top of the green folder that had been slid across the table top to her, Shaye waited for permission to open it. God had not spoken to her yet to allow her to do that. She was afraid of what she would read. And that fear was translating into tremors that shook her body. Slavin's arm around her was helping to some extent.

"What happened with that message, John? Could they just get rid of it?" Shaye wasn't that familiar with technology.

"It's possible, Shaye. We'll need to look over both of your phones. That we can do later. For now, we need to discuss what Frankie is here about." John knew that she was trying to delay the inevitable, the inevitable being opening that folder. He frowned as she just refused to remove her hand from on top of it.

"Shaye? What happened today?" Frankie kept his eyes on her, knowing that something had.

"I don't know. I was working away in the office all morning, just finishing up estimations that I have done. Samuel was in touch about one that I was to go to this afternoon. I cancelled it. He couldn't find the information that he needed to prove that it was safe." Shaye sighed, blowing out her breath. "And that's going to continue to happen, isn't it?"

"It likely will. You did right in asking Samuel to search the properties. Our feeling and the word on the street is that if you go out on one, you not likely will come home. You're to disappear. Only we don't know why. That is not obvious as of now." John turned to Slavin as he made a move. "Slavin?"

"They want her expertise. If she can undervalue a property, they pay less tax. If she overvalues a property, then they sell for a huge profit. It doesn't matter if it's right and correct. That's how they do it. Money laundering." Slavin's arm tightened around his lady.

"That's correct, Slavin. That's what we're hearing in my town." Frankie's finger tapped at the folder in front of Shaye. "This contains that information and who is likely involved. I'm sorry, Shaye. Emma has picked up on a couple of your fellow estimators. They've been running a scam for years now and for some reason have decided that you have found out about it and are trying to get you disqualified. We've spoken to who we need to speak with. At the moment, those two men are under arrest."

"Ant that will make it harder for me to say no, won't it? They'll suspect me." Shaye's face was solemn and troubled at the same time. All she could do was beg God to protect her somehow in her daily tasks.

"That's what we're hearing." John stared down at the folder in front of him, opening and then closing it. It was shoved towards Shaye, Slavin's hand coming out to rest on top of it. "This is a list of officers who will work with you. Don't hesitate to on any one of them even if it's to go to the grocery store. You'll disappear, Shaye. And we won't know where to find you. You will likely be removed from this town. We don't want that. You have friends here who would greatly miss you."

Shaye had not looked away from John as he spoke, not seeing the light yellow walls of her kitchen or the two-tone green paint of the cupboards. This had just gotten much worse.

"But how does Slavin fit in? They're going after him as well." Shaye turned slightly on her chair to face Slavin.

"That's another avenue that we're looking at, Shaye. Slavin is at risk as well. One, because you two are dating." John's hand went up at her protest. "You're a couple, whether you've acknowledged that or not. And secondly? His work as an archivist is finding information on that historical society and the ones behind the changes. I can't say what we've discovered as yet but there is a list of officers to work with Slavin as well. We are not walking away from either one of you. And if that doesn't work, we have three other security teams beside Peter's who will move in."

The two detectives walked away at last, stopping to speak with one another before they headed for their own vehicles. John sat and stared at the house that he had just left. He wasn't sure how much Shaye would use the list of officers but he prayed that she would. Word on the street was getting worse where she was concerned. Slavin? That was a whole other matter. He didn't seem to be facing the threats that Shaye was. No one could understand that, not as of yet.

Shaye turned from the sink, her hands reaching for a towel to dry them. She studied Slavin as he stood at the table, his eyes on the material that had been left.

"How do we do this, Slavin? How do we keep safe? We can't have someone with us all the time." Shaye was growing angrier at the disruption caused in her life.

"I don't know, sweetheart. I really don't know." Slavin looked up at that point. "I'm sorry. I really wanted to have lunch with you on our own."

"Yeah, about that. God had other plans." Shaye moved towards him, finding him just reaching to hug her. "I want this over, Slavin. How do we do that?"

"How do we do that? By researching. Peter is heading this way tonight, if it's okay. So are Sean, Roane and Skylor. Annie wants to bring a meal. And my parents are home and want to come to." He just held his lady, feeling her shaking for a moment.

"That's okay. We need to prepare for the onslaught." Shaye was away from him, heading for her office.

Slavin stared after her for a moment before he was following her, reaching for the photos and certificates that she was removing from the wall. His hands then reached to help tape paper to the walls.

Grinning at him for a moment, Shaye pointed to the walls and then to the folders.

"We can start, can't we?"

Slavin nodded, reaching to hug her once more before he pulled the box from his pocket.

<hr>

"Before we do, sweetheart, just let me speak. I am in love with you. I don't know how you feel though." Slavin watched as her eyes closed and a tear trickled down her cheek.

"I love you too, Slavin. I just thought that it was too soon." Shaye watched as he pulled a ring from the box. "Slavin?"

"Will you marry me, Shaye, soon? I am so afraid of you on your own." At her nod, he slid the rose gold ring with the emerald stone on her finger and then kissed her, holding her gently, his hold just telling her that she was loved and adored.

Chapter 27

His hand shaking as he reached for the red brick wall beside him, Slavin tried to pull himself to his feet. His hand kept slipping backwards as he just didn't have the strength to pull himself up. Slumping against the wall, Slavin searched the area around him, hardly able to see for the blurriness of his eyes. His assailants had disappeared and left him in a crumpled, battered, and bloody heap outside of his building. He had been taken unawares as he walked back to his office, his lunch in his hands. Slavin had had no chance to protect himself before he was down and being beaten.

Finally able to claw his way to his feet, Slavin swayed as he rested against the wall. He dug out his keys and stared at them, for the moment, his foggy brain unable to comprehend which key worked the lock for that door. He didn't hear the footsteps heading his way that paused and then proceeded towards him almost on a run.

"Slavin?" Nickol stood beside him, a hand gripping his upper arm to help keep him upright. "What happened to you?"

Slavin shrugged, not wanting to move his head. It hurt too much and he just knew that if he shook it, he would be down on the ground again.

"I'm not sure." He squinted at Nickol. "What are you doing here?"

"God. He sent me this way. I had such a burden for you just a bit ago." Nickol looked around, knowing that he couldn't enter the building, not having the password to the security system. His phone was out as he called for the emergency services.

Standing back from his from, Nickol watched as he was assessed and then wheeled away on a stretcher. Jerome stood beside him, consternation briefly on his face.

"Do you know what happened here, Nickol?" Jerome had to ask, even though he had a good idea that man wouldn't know.

"I don't know. I came up to him and found him leaning on the wall. He was really unsteady." Nickol looked around. "Someone is watching us and watching him too closely. There was no one around, I don't think, when this happened."

"Not likely. Or if there was, they are hiding. That happens. Word is out on the street that we want whoever it is that is after both Slavin and Shaye." Jerome paused as he studied Nickol. "Nickol?"

Nickol sighed. It wasn't his place to say anything but he had to.

"You're contacting his family?" At Jerome's nod, he waited for a moment. "Make sure that you call Shaye and get her to him. I spoke with her last night. They're engaged."

"They're what?" Jerome's words almost exploded from him before he swiped a hand down his face. "They just had to do that, didn't they?"

"They're in love, Jerome. And I for one will not stand in their way or condemn them. Who knows how long they have?" Nickol nodded towards the building. "This could have been much worse. I could have come upon his body and then had to explain to Shaye that he was dead. I don't want to be the one to do that." He walked away, his head turning as he did so. He caught the glimpse of a youth briefly showing himself and then disappearing. Nickol nodded to himself. Joey was coming through. He walked towards a local diner, heading for the office in there, something that he had done many times in the past. Joey would find him and then relay the information that the street had found for him.

Shaye stared in horror at Jerome as he stood in her front entryway. She had been working from home that day, finishing her reports and then scheduling estimations for the rest of the week. Her head began to shake in a negative way.

"I just spoke with him about thirty minutes ago. This can't be right." Shaye reached for her purse, locking her home behind her, Jerome's hand on her upper arm to help her walk.

"It is, Shaye. I'm sorry. Slavin was assaulted outside of his building. It looks as if he had gone to get his lunch. He never made it back inside. Nickol found him." Jerome watched her carefully as he sped off, heading for the Emergency department at their local hospital.

"That's why he didn't call. He said that he would call when he was on lunch. We were to meet with his family tonight." Shaye was out of Jerome's car and running inside the hospital, desperate to find Slavin.

———

She turned from speaking with the clerk, devastation on her face, to find Sean waiting for her.

Sean simply wrapped her into a hug before he turned her to where Annie was seated. Shaye's steps slowed as she saw the older couple on their feet, watching her.

"Your parents are here. I can't stay." Shaye would have run from there if Sean's arm had not been around her.

"You're part of our family, Shaye, no matter how it happened. Slavin has made his choice in you. God has brought you two together. I know that you haven't had a chance to meet Mom and Dad yet as they've been away. Come on. They won't bite." Sean had a small smile on his face as he uttered those last words, watching as Shaye took them in and then stared at him, shocked that he would say such a thing.

Stephen and Emily watched as Shaye was hesitant to approach them. They knew of her from their church activities and had briefly spoken to her at times. This was different, thought. She was Slavin's chosen lady. He had dropped by their home the night before, almost unable to keep his feet on the ground.

"Shaye?" Emily simply reached to hug the younger lady, holding on as she felt the suppressed sobs that Shaye would not allow to escape. "Welcome to our family. But have you heard anything?"

Shaye shook her head even as Stephen too reached to hug his son's lady. He was worried about her and worried about Slavin. He had no idea what had been going on or how dangerous it had become for the couple. All he could do at the present time was pray for them.

"No. I can't go back. You're his family. They'll let you." Shaye perched on the edge of a seat, sitting beside Emily.

"No, you're his family, Shaye. We'll all go back. For now, let's pray for him and for you." Stephen watched as Shaye's head turned to him.

"And for you as well. This is affecting too many people." Shaye's eyes closed as a single tear trickled down her cheek. This was not how her day was to have been. Slavin and she had had plans for that night, plans that had included a visit to his parents for a meal.

Chapter 28

Walking back towards where Slavin was, Shaye shook. She was so afraid for her fellow. Emily kept an arm around her, worried about the younger lady but worried about her son as well. They had no word on who or why other than Slavin was in danger. No one had come forward to state that they saw the assault. Stephen was sure that someone had but without proof, he didn't know who to approach.

Shaye's footsteps slowed as they entered the room. She moved away from Emily to find a corner to stand it, not sure if she should even be there. The declared love between the couple and their engagement was just too recent and fresh for Shaye to feel confident in it. Her gaze moved upwards as she begged God for protection for Slavin and peace and comfort for them both. They had chosen to live their lives even in danger with what they felt was God's blessings.

Stephen stood beside his son, watching as Slavin's head tossed from side to side. He could feel the anger rising within him, anger at whoever it was who had done this. He watched Shaye closely before he was beside her, an arm around her gently moving her forward to stand at the stretcher. Emily's hand was on her son's head, stilling the motion before it began again.

Shaye sighed, knowing that she had to react. But she was too afraid to do that. They were being watched, even here in the hospital. Someone was following them that close. John and Jerome had both been around, questioning them before they had found Slavin, only to find that he was still out of it as John put it and unable to tell them exactly what happened.

Her hand resting on Slavin's, Shaye felt the tremors that were wracking his body, tremors that she didn't understand. Slavin's eyes flickered open before they closed but the three with him could see the pain in them. Sean approached quietly, an arm around his mother. This was not what they had expected to face today. They had expected a quiet family dinner. This was definitely not that. Sean's prayer was for his brother and his lady, begging God to end whatever it was they were facing. He had no idea how to end it or he would do just that. Sean had had long conversations with both Peter and John, trying to understand exactly what to do. Neither of those men could help to any great degree.

Shaye walked away from Slavin, finding a corner to sit in. Her body crumpled against the walls as she fought her emotions. They were too raw for her to deal with adequately. Shaye was unable to pray, not knowing how to pray or what to ask for. She knew that the Holy Spirit prayed for them in that case, standing as an intermediary for them in these circumstances. Shaye looked up as someone sat near her, finding Annie just there for her.

"Shaye? What can we do for you?" Annie wasn't sure on what to ask or even what Shaye would need.

Shaye shrugged. She had no idea what was needed or how to ask for what she didn't know that she was in need of.

"I don't know, Annie. I truly don't know. Do you?" Shaye watched as Sean sat beside his wife, Stephen and Emily finding seats near the doors to the examination rooms.

"I don't know, Shaye. I really don't. You and Slavin are the first that we have had face this." Annie shared a look with Sean. "And that makes it difficult to know what to say or even how to say it. We are praying for you. That's a given."

"And I thank you for that." Shaye drew in a deep breath. "We need to meet again, I think, and just go over everything that we have. I've been trying to but it is so overwhelming. Slavin will want to be part of that." She frowned at the wall beside her. "I feel like I have walked into this wall and it just isn't going anywhere at all."

"We know, Shaye." Sean nodded, his eyes narrowing as he thought through her request. He didn't pay attention to those around him, his focus on Shaye. "Slavin will likely be in overnight. He'll want to be where you are when he's released. Do you have any appointments for the rest of the week?"

Shaye shook her head. She had cut back on what she was doing, trusting Samuel to guide her where she needed him to.

"No, not really. An urgent one may come up. I just don't feel safe going into homes or buildings. Not when we don't know why or who." She was on her feet as Emily approached her. "Emily?"

"Slavin's awake and is trying to get up when he shouldn't. He's looking for you." Emily's arm around Shaye led that lady back to where Slavin was struggling against his father and John to rise. "Slavin. Behave. Shaye is here and safe."

Slavin squinted at his lady before his hand reached for hers, drawing her close enough so that he could wrap an arm around her.

"You're okay? I was so worried about you." His voice held the worry that he wouldn't admit to.

"I'm fine. You're the one who seems to not be." Shaye studied him for a moment. "Who did this to you?"

Slavin shrugged, sitting up on the stretcher. He was adamant that he was going home that night and that Shaye had to be with him. That meant going to either his brother's or his parents' home. His parents won, with Slavin not wanting to bring any danger to his nephew.

"I don't know. I was blindsided and down before I saw who it was. And the security cameras in the area were destroyed. John told me that." Slavin drew in a deep breath, the pain rising within him. "How do we do this, Shaye? How do we keep you safe?"

"It's not just me, Slavin." Shaye pushed away from him, pacing the room. "It's you too. You need to stay safe and I don't know how we can do that. They seem to find us no matter where we are."

Slavin watched as Shaye walked away from him. He sighed as he lifted his eyes to look at the ceiling. He didn't know where she had gone but she was likely in danger. And Slavin was in no condition to protect her. That much he knew.

Nodding as his father's hand came out to steady him on his feet, Slavin almost shuffled from the room and out of the hospital. His eyes were searching for Shaye, not seeing her. That troubled him but at the moment he was in no shape to hunt for her. Sean studied him and then the area around them, seeing Shaye standing nearby and watching Slavin before she walked away, heading for a taxi and likely her home. He promised himself that he would find her that night.

Chapter 29

Shaye found her comfort spot on her couch and curled up under a blanket. She was cold even though the house was warm. Fear was doing that to her. When she had been found earlier that day, Shaye was certain that Slavin was dead. Her hand reached for her Bible, knowing that she would find comfort and peace there in God's Word. She just didn't see how they could solve whatever this was that they were involved in. And that needed to be done.

Her phone chiming startled her an hour later. She had been lost in thought, not sure where she was heading, but so afraid for Slavin. It wasn't clear which one of them it was or if it was both of them. She had spoken at length with Jerome and he could not answer that question, his comment being that whoever it was? They were keeping to the shadows.

Swiping across her phone screen to access it, Shaye read Slavin's message. She gave a small sad smile, knowing that she was walking away from the love of her life. She had to, she felt. Shaye didn't respond, simply setting her phone to one side. She had not words to speak with him.

Slavin waited somewhat impatiently for Shaye to respond. When she didn't, he pulled the covers up tighter around his neck. He had no idea who had beaten him that day. His only concern was Shaye and that lady just wasn't speaking with him.

Early the next morning, Peter was at Shaye's door, ringing the doorbell. Two of his men were outside. The other three were with Slavin. John had asked him to move in just for the next few days and Peter and his team had been agreeable.

Shaye stared at him before she turned and walked away, heading for her bedroom and a chance to clean up. She had spent the night on the couch and that hadn't started her day off very well. That and the fact that Peter was there so early in the morning.

Peter shook his head before he headed for the kitchen, reaching to make the pot of coffee that was needed and then searching for food to make Shaye's breakfast. It was not the first time he had done something like that for someone his team was protecting and not likely would be the last.

Shaye stood with her hand on her bedroom door knob, knowing that when she left that room, things would change. And that change scared her. She reached for her phone and scrolled through her messages, both personal and business. A frown crossed her face at the urgent request for an estimation that needed to be done that day. Shaye was not familiar with that mortgage broker.

"Peter? I have a request to do an urgent estimation today." Shaye stood in her kitchen, a frown on her face.

"And that troubles you?" Peter reached for her phone, reading the message and then forwarding it to himself and also John and Jerome. "You're not certain on this name?"

"No, I'm not. I know the brokers and agents in town. He says he's from here but I have never heard of him." Shaye looked at him, fear in her eyes. "Is this a set-up?"

Peter was nodding, knowing that Shaye was reading the message correctly.

"I would suspect it is. I'll have one of the guys go by there and check out the property. Don't respond just yet." Peter was away, sending one man from Shaye's and one from Slavin's to head to that address. He suspected that it was a set-up but he needed proof of that before he would let Shaye head that way.

An hour later, Peter strode towards Shaye's home office, startling her for a moment with the sound of his footsteps. She decided that she didn't like the look on his face.

"Peter? What did you find out?" Shaye watched as Peter paced her office.

"It is a set-up, Shaye. My guys were there, keeping out of sight, and watched the men walking the property. We know them. I have spoken with Jerome and John and they were moving in to arrest them." His hand went up as her mouth opened. "It's what we do, Shaye. They'll sort it all out. Has he come back with any messages?"

Shaye nodded, her phone held out to Peter.

"He has. And they are getting nastier as time passes. What have I gotten involved in?" Shaye's question didn't have an answer at the moment. All she could do was pray that it soon would and there were no guarantees of that.

"He is getting nasty. Slavin was asking about you." Peter watched with compassion in his eyes as Shaye refused to meet his gaze. "He's worried about you. Being engaged? That changes how you both think about one another. And don't try to pack up and run. Slavin will follow you. That would put you both at greater risk."

Shaye nodded, having come to that conclusion. She sank back in her chair, her eyes on Peter as he watched her.

"I get that, Peter. I just don't want to be the one who caused all this for him."

"I don't think that you are. Someone is after each one of you. I suspect that there is someone behind both of them, directing what they are doing." Peter found a chair and sat, waiting for Shaye to think that through and then respond to him.

"That's what I feel. How do we do this? How do we find them?" Shaye reached for a pen and pad of paper. "I was trying to come up with names last night and did. I don't know if Slavin would have the same names."

"It's possible. I did ask him to do that, to make a list. His mom said that he was asleep early and wasn't awake yet." Peter shook his head. "His body needs to heal, Shaye. What he went through yesterday? It caused trauma. Both of you are victims of violence and crime. We need to do what we can to protect you and also solve this. A friend is weighing in on the search. She thought that she would have information today for me. Can I pass on your email address to her? She'll send what she can to you as well. If she sends something, she will have proven that information."

Shaye shrugged, not sure on that but agreeable to Peter's request if it meant solving whatever this was.

"Sure. I guess. It's needed. Samuel is searching the properties that I need to estimate. I have cut back on that for now. I just don't want to put anyone at risk." Shaye turned to her computer as she heard a chime. "And Samuel has gotten back to me already about that property in the message. As far as he can determine, it is not for sale and never has been. We were right. It was a set-up."

"And you would have gone in and disappeared, if this had not happened to you. You are being cautious and I like that. Not everyone is." Peter was on his feet as he heard a tap at the door, opening it to find Sean and Slavin standing there. That did not surprise him. What surprised him was seeing the rest of Slavin's family walking towards them. "You're all here?"

"We are, Peter. John wants us all together. They have been receiving threats against us. Jerome is in agreement with that. It makes it easier for us to be protected, they think." Slavin moved past him, looking for his lady, not liking the stress that he saw on her face before he simply wrapped her into a hug.

Peter nodded as he watched Emily and Annie head for the kitchen with their bags of food. He was not surprised when Andrew made a lunge for him from his father's arms. Children were like that with him.

"We're working in the office, people. Let's see what we can determine today to move this investigation ahead." Peter stepped outside to speak with his team, sending them around the house. He didn't want any surprises that day.

Chapter 30

Slavin raised his head at last. It was mid-afternoon and they had all been deep into the investigation. He wasn't sure where they stood in it. On his feet, Slavin headed for the front door, stepping outside and then stretching. He studied the area around Shaye's home, liking it more and more. It suited him better than his own home did. Slavin turned as he heard a voice talking to him and frowned. He didn't know the man standing there but Peter seemed to.

"Slavin? This is Richard. He's a friend but also has a security team. I asked him to stop by, just to help us determine how to protect you two." Peter grinned up at Slavin before he was climbing the steps, Richard following him.

"Good to meet you, Slavin. And yes, my team, my brother and my wife's brother all had what we consider adventures. So, we can speak from experience." Richard studied the man in front of him and then the lady who had stopped beside Slavin.

Slavin's arm wrapped around Shaye. She had come to find him, needing that contact with him.

"Richard? You're here?" Shaye reached to hug the tall man who stood on her porch. "Peter called you."

"He did, Shaye. I hear you're not finding out too much about what is happening." Richard grinned at the disgruntled look on her face before his head was bowed and he was praying for the couple. Slavin frowned as Richard gave his usual "I love You" instead of an amen. "What can we do for you two?"

"Solve this. We need to do that, Richard." Shaye paced around her porch, finally coming back to stand in front of Peter and Richard. "How do we do that? And no, we are not running away or hiding away anywhere. That never solves anything."

"No, you're correct. It doesn't. It just prolongs it." Richard watched as Peter walked away. "Just for the record, Slavin? Shaye and my wife, Raleigh, are friends. They met at a conference and have kept in touch. So, what all do you not know?"

Slavin frowned at Richard's phrasing and then at his grin. He shrugged. Give him something archival to investigate and he knew how to do that. This? It had him stumped.

"I really don't know what I don't know." Slavin didn't catch the grins that crossed Shaye's and Richard's faces. "Maybe you can see something that we're missing." He sighed. "I want this over yesterday."

Richard nodded. Slavin was at the point that everyone who had such an adventure reached.

"Peter says that you're investigating the historical society?"

"I am and I have reached an impasse in that. There is information being changed. I have a hunch as to who it is. I just can't prove it yet." Slavin was greatly troubled by that, having to go to God with his concerns and worry and finding the peace that only

God could give. "We want to live our lives, Richard. This, whatever this is, is standing in our way."

"It can. Or you can decide to live the life that God has chosen for you and make your plans." Richard studied Slavin, seeing just when that man understood what he was saying.

Slavin nodded, his arm reaching to draw Shaye close to him. He wanted to go ahead with their plans but he also didn't want to rush Shaye. He wanted her to enjoy the life of an engaged and cherished lady before they took that step of marriage.

"I get what you are saying, Richard. We'll talk, Shaye and I." Slavin bit at his bottom lip before he looked up at the clear blue sky. "What would you do to advance the investigation? John and Jerome are working it but they have other cases as well."

"I know that they do. Lead me to where you're working and I'll see what I can do." Richard followed them into the house, looking around. He liked the comfort of Shaye's home. It was a home where one could live and love and grow as a family.

Shaye looked around late that evening, studying the piles of paper that were neatly stacked on her dining room table and then walked through to her office, to study the paper that Richard has insisted needing to be on the walls. She smiled as she remembered the grin that he had given her when he stated that everyone always ended up doing that.

Slavin had taken a reluctant leave from her, a tight and long hug delivered as well as a kiss good-night. Shaye smiled as she remembered the reluctancy with which he had walked away, turning back to stare at her, a smile on his face. She had no idea what she was to do with him, other than marry him and quickly. Slavin didn't want that, he stated. He wanted her to enjoy being engaged, well as much as she could given the danger that they found themselves in.

Slavin sank down into his bed, his eyes closing even as he pulled up the covers. He was chilled, and he knew that was from pain and stress. He had overdone it, he decided, that day but he had not wanted to walk away from his lady. They had made progress, he decided, but they still had to determine just who is was and why.

Early the next morning, Slavin was at his desk in his office building, reaching to wake up his computer and access his email. Working through the requests, his hand stopped as he reached the last one. Slavin frowned. He didn't know this person but they had reached out to him. Just who was Jacob Whitson? He was a friend of Richard's, he stated. Richard had spoken to him. Finn, his wife, ran an antique store that deal with old books and documents. Could they help in some way?

Slavin's eyes slid closed. This was exactly what was needed. Someone from outside to take a look at what was going on. Richard had also recommended another friend of his, a man by the name of Noah, who did ethical hacking. Slavin had reached out to him at Richard's insistence and Noah had agreed to take a look at what was happening with the historical society's website. Slavin was afraid of what Noah would find but if he found anything, then that would explain what he himself was finding.

Shaye stared at the officer in front of her, a man preventing her from leaving her home. She frowned at him before she closed the door and locked it. She was not familiar with that officer. Something seemed off about his uniform as well. Shaye peeked through the window as she called John, simply asking if he knew an officer by the name of Ted Lang.

John was on his feet. He had just come across that name. That man was not an officer but was an assassin. If he was at Shaye's, then she was in deeper trouble than they thought.

The man turned as he heard the sirens and ran for his car, not making it in time. A patrol vehicle cut in front of him and stopped him in his tracks. Handcuffed, the man was shoved into a vehicle even as John ran towards the house, hammering at the door for Shaye to open it.

Shaye didn't respond. She couldn't. She was no longer in her house and free. The back door had flown open and she was tackled to the floor, her hands bound behind her before she was hauled roughly to her feet and then shoved through the back door, the door hanging awkwardly on its hinges.

John stared at the open door before he was through it, officers following him, their hands on their weapons as they searched. He stood outside on the back deck, afraid for Slavin's lady. She had disappeared and he had no idea where she would be and he doubted that the man in custody would speak.

———

Chapter 31

Slavin stared at John, his hands clasped behind his neck, shock on his face as he tried to take in what John was saying. His head shook. Shaye could not have disappeared. That wasn't possible. He had spoken with her not even an hour before and they had made plans.

"I'm sorry, Slavin. Shaye is missing. Someone broke into her home and took her. We arrested someone posing as an officer on her property. We think that her disappearance and this man are connected but we don't know for sure." John walked away after a time, not satisfied that he had accomplished anything other than for scaring Slavin. He had no answers for his friend. His head lifted as he studied the rain clouds that were gathering, a fitting scene, he decided. All he could do was pray for Shaye, for her protection, and then for Slavin and his family. Not one person had an answer for him, not even Emma. And that was unusual, he knew.

Slavin stared after John, devastation on his face. It couldn't be true, he decided, heading for Shaye's home and seeing the yellow police tape around it. He sank back against his truck, praying hard for his lady. They had planned to take the afternoon and make some decisions. That wasn't happening now. Slavin frowned as he heard footsteps stop beside and looked sideways. Peter stood there and Slavin could see his team spreading out in the near vicinity.

"Slavin?" Peter spoke at last, his eyes not on the man beside him but on the surrounding area. He could feel the evil that kept creeping closer to his friend and prayed hard for him.

"Shaye's gone, Peter. And I don't know where or who." Slavin sighed, slumping back against his vehicle. "John found me and told me that. We don't know when that happened."

"I see. Come with me, Slavin. Leave your keys for Simon. He'll bring your vehicle to you. For now, we need to get you out of sight." Peter's hand had a tight grip on Slavin's upper arm, not letting him escape and stay where he was. "We need to do this, Slavin. This is not helping us find your lady."

Slavin finally nodded, following John as he walked away, his team closing in around them. Simone took the proffered keys and headed for Slavin's vehicle, hesitating for a moment before he was searching it, not liking what he was finding. He was on his feet, heading for a patrol officer nearby who stared at him in horror before he was calling for the bomb squad. This was not what Slavin needed at this time.

Peter turned from where he had been contemplating Slavin's front yard, nodding as he saw the security that had been set up. Someone had done that for him. Most of his team were outside, only Paul inside with Slavin, who had objected at that until Peter stared him down.

"Simon? What was there?" Peter knew something had been. It had taken too long for Simon to appear and to appear from a patrol vehicle was not what he had expected.

"There was a bomb on his car, Peter. We think that it was likely planted even as he leaned against the vehicle. Someone was that close to him. And I want to know why." Simon was angry and that was not him, not to show his anger.

Peter stared at him before he nodded.

"It's what we've been expecting. Only we don't know why. Or do we?" Peter had a thought, his hand out to pull Simon with him. "Simon, your speciality is investigations. This is who we need to investigate. And get that name to Emma as well." He watched as Simon asked Slavin to use his computer and then that man began to work through their protocol to reach the sites that he needed.

Slavin approached Peter, seeing Sean, Roane, and Nickol standing there.

"What did you find, Peter? My car's not here." Slavin tamped down his anxiety and fear, wanting answers and wanting them that day. He knew that God was in control and had sheltered him from harm sometime that day.

"A bomb, Slavin. A bomb was planted, likely Simon thinks as you were standing and leaning against your car. Did you hear or see anything?" Peter knew that John would be around, asking those questions. He couldn't wait for that. He needed to know in order to decide how best to protect Slavin. At this point in time, Slavin had just gone into protective custody.

Slavin stared at him in horror. He had not heard or seen anyone. That scared him, to tell the truth. He heard the murmurs from the three other men.

"A bomb? Who?"

"We don't know. For now, we're with you. If we can't be, another team moves in." Peter walked away, his phone out to contact Richard, who was agreeable to move in as was Richard's friends, Don and Abe. It was what they did for one another.

Slavin nodded before he turned from the office, seeking to find somewhere that he could pray. He found his prayer corner in his conservatory, sinking down into a wicker chair, knowing that his brother had followed him, just to stand with him in his desperate attempt to understand what was happening. And that he just could not do.

Slavin raised his head at last, feeling peace in his heart. He looked over at Sean, finding his brother watching him closely.

"Sean? What would you do if this was Annie?" Slavin waited patiently for his brother to speak.

"What would I do?" At Slavin's nod, Sean thought through what his brother was asking. "I would be out there, openly searching for her. I would be putting word out on the street that I want whoever this is. This has gone on long enough, Slavin. You need to end it. Roane has some information that he wants to share with you. Nickol has been working with him. And I understand that Simon has been finding information that he is confirming. It doesn't bring

———

Shaye home. All we can do is surround her with our prayers.”

Slavin nodded, knowing what his brother was not saying. Shaye may not come home in a way that they liked. And that troubled him greatly. He wanted to start a life with her. Only at the moment, he wasn’t sure that they would even get that chance. Slavin was on his feet, heading for the office and to hear what his friends had to say.

Chapter 32

The day that she disappeared, Shaye had been bound and a gag slapped over her mouth. She had been forcefully removed from her home, dragged through the broken back door and then through her yard and a few neighbouring yards before she was shoved into a car. She struggled to escape, not able too, blows to her arms and back bringing deep pain to her. The men who had taken her captive didn't care that it was a lady that they were hitting. The depravity of their souls showed in their actions.

Shaye was hauled forcefully once more from the vehicle and then shoved ruthlessly into a room in the centre of the house that they had arrived at. She had been too scared to take in much of the looks of the house, wanting to escape and just not able to do so. The key grated loudly in the lock, shutting her into the room. Her bonds had been released but not the gag.

Her hands on the gag, Shaye tore it from her mouth, retching as she did so. The horrible taste from the dirty rag lingered as she swiped at her mouth, searching for any source of water. Spying the sink in a two-piece ensuite, Shaye was there, bent over it, desperately rinsing out her mouth with the cold water. She continued to retch even as she did so. Finally, she raised to her full height, finding a new cloth on the counter. Shaye wrung it out in as hot of water as she could stand, her face scrubbed with it.

Returning to the room, Shaye stared around and then began a systematic search for a way to escape or for anything to defend herself. She found neither. She was growing more and more frightened as each moment passed. She had no idea as to why she had been taken.

The day drew to a close and then night also passed. A bag of food had been dropped inside the door, with Shaye only able to see the man's hand as he did so. The door was locked before she could even think to try and escape.

Days passed like this until a week had gone by. That day, Shaye was dragged from the room even as she protested and then demanded answers. The man had refused to respond. Instead, he had slammed her down onto a hard armless wooden chair and then stood with his hands pressing down on her shoulders, preventing her from rising.

The door behind her opened once more and Shaye sensed evil in the room with her. She refused to look up at the man as his shuffling steps stopped in front of her, a small table separating them. The man, wizened and old, his clothes ill fitting, stared at her. His angry glare didn't move from her. Shaye would do what he wanted. She was never returning home and would never seen Slavin or any of his family again. That much he had determined. He really didn't care if she lived or died.

The man stood for close to an hour, not saying a word. He frowned as Shaye's face remained blank and she didn't look at him or react in any way at all as he stood there. He finally waved at the man to return her to her cell, for that was what it was, a cell holding her captive.

———

Shaye retreated across the room, standing at a window, her breath coming in hard gasps. She was terrified. She didn't know the man who had stood there but she had felt the evil emanating from him. He didn't mean her health, that much she knew. Shaye grew desperate to escape. Only there seemed to be no way for that to happen.

Studying the windows, Shaye's eyes narrowed. They were old wooden windows, not really in that great of shape. She began to pick away at the wood around the nails, finding it loosening. She shot a glance behind her at the locked door and then sighed. Even if she got the wood around the nails enough to loosen them, there was the problem of raising the window. The frame was swollen and old. Shaye just didn't know if she could raise it and escape. God was not letting her do that, not yet. It may come that He would but until He did, she stayed where she was.

The next week went on as that day had. Shaye was forced to sit in the same chair with the same man holding her there. The old man would appear and just stand to watch her, frustrated that Shaye was showing no emotions and certainly not the fear that he expected from her.

On the fifteenth day of her captivity the man changed. He strode into the room, albeit his stride shaky. He had been imbibing of the liquor that he liked, trying to find the courage to make his demands, demands that he had no idea if she would follow or not. It was up to Shaye whether she lived or died, he decided, depending on her response to him.

———

Shaye refused to look up, keeping her eyes on her clasped hands in her lap. Her face remained neutral. It was only God that helped her to stay that way. In her humanness she would have reacted and that would have gone badly for her.

The man stared at her, a frown in place. He could not understand why Shaye was not reacting. Anyone else would have done his bidding by the third day. This was now day eight.

"You will work with me, young lady. And that starts today." His fist hammered at the table. He continued to frown as there was no response from Shaye, not even a flicker of an eyelid. That bothered him. Everyone always responded. "Do you hear me? You will start working for me today."

When Shaye still refused to look up or respond, the man stared at her before he finally stomped from the room, waving at the man to return her to her cell.

Shaye drew in a deep breath once the door locked behind her. She was afraid and deeply afraid at that. She was praying hard for release but that didn't seem to be happening. No one likely knew where she was and that frightened her, to be alone without any human companionship or help. She could only pray for her beloved Slavin and his family, begging God to keep them safe.

The next day, Shaye was once more slammed down into the chair, barely keeping herself from reacting. The man who had moved her there on a daily basis was puzzled. He too could not figure out why Shaye was not responding. He looked around as he felt a presence in the room but saw no one. His eyes moved to Shaye and saw the shape in front of her, between Shaye and the table. He rubbed at his eyes and the shape disappeared. What had that been, he wondered? His conscience began to prick at him. He was only a new hire and didn't like the man he was working for. The more he learned about him, the more he wanted to run. But something kept him there or rather someone. And that someone was Shaye. He would not and could not abandon her.

Chapter 33

That day, the old man's shuffling and dragging footsteps sounded loud in Shaye's ears. There was something different about them, she thought, more frail and feeble than even the day before. Hope began to grow within her that she would be able to flee. That was until she heard the second set of footsteps, younger and more stable. That frightened her. She refused to look up at the men on the other side of the table and refused to let any emotion sit on her face or in her eyes. She had learned to hide her emotions early in life. That had been driven into her by her parents, even though they professed to love her. She had walked away from them when she was sixteen, finding the freedom that she cherished. An older couple from the church had taken her in and helped her to learn to live life as a free lady.

The old man stared at Shaye and then at the man beside him, a frown deepening on his face. He needed Shaye to decide that day if she would work for him. If not, then she would disappear and her body would never be found. She would be grieved but there was not his concern.

"You will work for me!" His words reverberated in the room, the volume almost too loud.

The men with him winced as the volume just increased each time he repeated that sentence. They stared at Shaye as she just sat there, not moving and not responding.

The old man stared at her and then at the younger man beside him. He had made plans that included the two of them.

"And you will marry my son!" This was shouted at Shaye. He stared in shock as she just continued to sit there, a mist or what seemed to be a mist separating her from him.

The younger man stared at the old man in horror. He rarely saw the man who claimed him as his son. This was in fact not the case. He was a young man who lived in the house next door and avoided the old man at all times that were possible.

"I'm not your son!" The younger man didn't raise his voice but his was a commanding tone that stopped the old man. "I am not your son. And I will not marry this lady. She already has someone she loves and who loves her. What have you done?" He was away from the room, almost on a run, before he could be stopped.

The old man glared after him and then at the man standing behind Shaye, shock on his face as well as the hatred he felt for all men and women. He began to shake, his fists hammering at the table.

The man standing behind Shaye stared at him and then down at Shaye before he grabbed for her and pulled her to her feet, running from the room. He ignored the shouts to stop and come back that hammered the air after him. He paused long enough to swing the door closed and turn the key in the lock, not knowing how long they would have to escape.

Shaye ran with the man, her hand tight in hers. She could feel a hand on her back, shoving her forward even though there was no one behind her. She looked up briefly, mouthing a thank you to her Heavenly Father before her focus was on her escape.

The man shoved her into his car and then ran for his own seat, speeding away and heading for the police department. Enough was enough, he decided. He needed to let Shaye out there and then flee the town. That man would never rest until he was found and dealt with. And being dealt with in that old man's book meant that he died.

Shaye stared at her rescuer, not sure what to say or think. She then stared at the police building, shocked that he had brought her there.

"Go on, Shaye. Go on in. You're free. That young man? He'll speak with the police. The old guy? For now, he's locked in that room. He doesn't have a key to get out. The night guard will be around soon. Just be very careful. He'll be out for revenge because you wouldn't work for him and then because you escaped. No one has ever done that."

Shaye looked at the man, seeing for the first time just how young he was.

"What about you? You're not safe." Shaye began to worry about him.

"I'll be okay. I'm headed away from here." The man hesitated for a moment. "Who was that who was standing between you and the table? I saw a form."

"It was an angel sent by God to protect me. Plain and simple, He does that at times." Shaye reached to squeeze the man's hand that rested on the gear stick. "Search for Him, please. He will be found." Shaye turned and then was out of the car, running towards John who had just appeared at the door to the building.

"Shaye? What? Where did you come from?" John hustled her back into the building and then to his office. "Where have you been?"

"I have a story to tell, John, but first. There is an old man locked in his office at this address. He's the one who kidnapped me and kept me from escaping. Arrest him, please. I don't know that I will live if he's still out there. And once you've taken care of that, I'll talk." Shaye brushed at the tears gathering in her eyes. "Is there any chance of a coffee? I've only had bread and water the last few days. I need something to keep me going."

John nodded, stepping to the doorway as one of the other detectives approached. That lady nodded. She knew Shaye and knew that Shaye would want fresh clothes. She was back with the coffee, a quiet word to John as she left to find just those clothes for her friend.

"Okay, Shaye, talk to me. I want to know where you were and why." John sat beside her, not across the desk from her. She needed that, he decided.

Shaye sipped at her coffee before she nodded.

"Slavin? He's okay?" Her voice was low and broken. She had convinced herself that he was either dead or had moved on from her.

"He's hurting, Shaye, just because you were gone. We'll get you to him in a bit. But first, who was that who dropped you off?" John waited patiently for Shaye to speak, nodding at Jerome as he entered and found a seat.

Shaye began to speak, telling everything that had happened, what she had felt, how she had coped, and the despair that had claimed her. She frowned at John as she told about the man who had stood in front of her every time that she was in the office.

"An angel, John. God sent an angel to protect me." Shaye saw him nodding as did Jerome. It was not the first time that they had heard of something like this.

"Let's get you cleaned up, Shaye. Then, we'll find Slavin. We've been trying hard to come up with answers for what you two have faced. This explains what you were going through, but it doesn't explain Slavin's troubles." John hesitated for a moment, his mouth open to ask a question when Shaye spoke once more.

"I think that you'll find there is someone behind this man. That someone is also behind what Slavin is facing. Somehow, we're tied together in a way that we have not yet discovered. And I want to know who and why." Shaye was on her feet, heading for her detective friend and then a shower and clean clothes. She needed to find Slavin and find him as soon as she could.

Chapter 34

Hearing a tap at his back door, Slavin was on his feet, moving from where he had been in the living room. He was discouraged and down that night, not expecting Shaye to ever return. He frowned as the tap came again. Slavin had no idea who would be at his back door. Everyone always came to the front door.

Opening the door, Slavin just stood, a hand on the door, as he stared at the beautiful lady in front of him. Shaye stood as well, her eyes on his beloved face, not moving towards him, not sure if she was still the love of his life.

"Shaye?" Slavin could hardly see for the tears in his eyes. "You're home. God has brought you back to me." He reached for her, finding her moving his way, their arms around each other. He felt a hand moving them into the house before the door closed.

John stood on the back deck, his eyes on the stars that were starting to shine. He could only thank God that He had brought Shaye back home. That was not something that anyone had expected. They had all expected that she was either moved out of the country or dead.

Slavin finally stood back enough that he could watch Shaye's beautiful face. He could see the subtle changes in it, changes that he didn't like. She stared up at him, in wonder once more at his height. Shaye had been so afraid that he was dead. That was what that man had kept hitting her with.

"I thought that you were dead." Shaye simply moved back into his space, her arms clinging to him, her tears soaking his flannel shirt.

"And I thought that about you." Slavin turned them to the living room, finding his favourite chair and pulling her down into it with him. "Can you tell me what happened?"

"I can. It's not pretty, Slavin. Not at all. I just don't know why that man was reacting as he was." Shaye's head rested against her beloved fellow. She then proceeded to tell her story, finding his arms tightening around her.

"He really expected you to marry that man?" Slavin was in shock.

"He did. John, I think, was moving in on them. I just don't know how safe we are or why." Shaye sighed, her prayers deepening for peace and understanding of what was going on with them. "I choose life, Slavin." Her hand was held up, the light from the nearby lamp reflecting from her ring. "We need to move forward with our plans."

"We do, sweetheart. We do. Mom has been pushing for that. She simply stated that you were coming home and that we needed to marry." Slavin gave a quick grin before his heart raised his prayers of thankfulness and for peace and understanding in what they were facing. "Tomorrow?"

Shaye lifted her head to stare at him, finding him not looking at her. His focus was straight ahead of him, not sure if she would even agree to that.

"Tomorrow, it is." Shaye sighed. "I need to go, Slavin. John's waiting for me." She was on her feet and away from him, leaving him standing and staring after her.

Slavin's head dropped for a moment before he was to the front door, watching as John tucked Shaye into his vehicle, a hand raised to wave at his friend. He watched the car disappear down the street before he was back inside, reaching for his phone.

"Mom? Shaye's home." Slavin blinked back tears as he heard his mother's voice and her sob as she understood what he was saying. "We want to marry tomorrow. Can we do that?"

"You're both sure?" Stephen's voice could be heard over the airwaves.

"We are, Dad. This separation took too much from us. Shaye said that the man who held her wanted her to marry someone. She ran at that point. And yes, John and Jerome are working on that." Slavin moved through his house to his bedroom, opening his closet to find his suit. He had made plans for flowers and a meal, not knowing if that would ever happen.

"Then, we do this." Emily reached for her own phone, heading away, hearing Stephen praying with his son. She reached out to Shaye, not sure of that lady would even answer her call. "Shaye? We are so glad you're home. I won't say safe."

Shaye gave a brief, brittle laugh at that.

"No, I can't say that we're safe. We have the one who kidnapped me but not the one behind him or whoever it is that is after Slavin." Shaye curled up on her couch, a sober look on her face. She needed things for the next day and just didn't have them.

"I understand, Shaye. Now, about tomorrow? You don't have a dress, do you?" Emily heard the sob that Shaye just could not control. "We can meet at the bridal store early. I know the lady who runs it. She will gladly open for us. Or there is my dress."

"I think the shop, Emily, if you don't mind." Shaye hesitated. "Thank you, Mom. I need a mom and mine is no longer in my life. You're stepping in." She closed off the call before Emily could respond.

Emily blinked back tears from her eyes, feeling Stephen's arms around her. They both prayed for the couple, knowing that this step would likely trigger even more danger. They just didn't know who, no matter how much everyone had been working on it. That person was staying hidden and that didn't help relieve their minds of worry.

Early the next morning, Shaye walked towards Emily as she stood on the sidewalk outside of her home. Emily simply reached to hold the lady her son loved and then tucked her into her car.

"You're sure about this, Shaye?" Emily just had to ask.

"We are, Mom. We are." Shaye refused to look at that lady, thinking that she would see censure and dislike. She was not prepared for Emily to just reach for her hand and pray for her new daughter.

"Then, let's go have some fun. It's Saturday. Andrew is with his father. Annie wanted to meet us."

"That's fine." Shaye finally looked over at Emily. "I always wanted a sister or a really close friend and had neither. Annie is picking that up for me."

Chapter 35

Slavin turned from where he stood in his parents' living room, finding Shaye walking towards him. He drew in a deep breath. She was already a beautiful lady but the lacy white gown of a simple design that the ladies had found that morning just seemed to bring out more of her beauty. His hand reached for hers, his grip strong and true, as they turned back to their pastor.

Late that night, Slavin wandered his home, hearing Shaye moving around in the kitchen and putting away what they had brought home in food. He stood for a moment outside of the kitchen doorway, watching her before he simply moved in on her to kiss her and then hug her. Slavin was deeply afraid for his lady, knowing that someone was still out there. They had seen signs of that outside of his parents' home and then here at their home.

Shaye sighed to herself. Slavin was trying too hard to protect her, not looking at his own safety. That had to change. Only she had no way of knowing how to do just that.

"Slavin? Sweetheart? What do we do? How do we find out who is behind this?" Shaye tightened her hug on her groom.

"I don't know, my love. I really don't know. Peter wants to meet with us again tomorrow night. He's bringing in Richard and Don, he says." Slavin turned them towards his office, finding their prayer corner. "We need to pray, my love. It's only going to get worse from here on out."

"I know. I want this over with. It's gone on for too long." Shaye wiped at her eyes, hating that she was once more in tears. She never wept. Today? She felt overwhelmed and terrified.

"I do too." Slavin reached for his Bible, searching for the verses that would bring comfort to them. He looked up at last, searching Shaye's face. "Shaye? What are your thoughts?"

"My thoughts? About who it is?" At his nod, Shaye sank back against her chair, her eyes not leaving his face. "This is who." She began to name people, almost speaking too rapidly for Slavin to write them down. "And we need to narrow that down. How do we do that?"

"I reach out to Emma and give her this list. I won't yet to John. He's got enough on his plate without knowing for certain who to look for." Slavin set aside the paper, reaching for Shaye and drawing her to his knee. "For now, let's set it aside. We need to do that."

"We do. We're too close to what is happening to be objective, aren't we?" Shaye's arm was around Slavin's neck. "So, we leave it for someone else to determine. We begin to live our lives."

"And we will. We are choosing life, aren't we?" Slavin grinned at his bride before he kissed her. "And that begins tomorrow. We no longer hide. We are out and about doing what we would normally be doing to live that life."

———

"We are. God is our Protector. Nothing happens to us that is not in His will for us." Shaye sighed once more. "Only, in our humanness, we want to take that over."

"We do and we can to a certain extent. We are cautious where we go and who we are around. We watch for those people and those who we know work for them. We are around our families." Slavin studied Shaye for a moment. "You never speak much about yours."

Shaye shook her head.

"As far as they are concerned, I'm dead to them. I no longer care if they are alive or dead. I have had to give them to God. That took a lot to do. But I have peace that He will deal with them." She studied Slavin for a moment. "Do you think that they are involved in any way?"

Slavin shrugged. That had been his thought at one point but now? He wasn't sure what to think. He had asked Emma to search them out just the day before and she had promised to do that. She didn't tell him that she already had and that they were dead. That was a conversation that she wanted to have with the couple in person.

The next day, during the late afternoon, Shaye turned from her office desk. She had been at work there most of the day, disturbed at the emails that she was receiving. She had forwarded them on to John and Jerome. On her feet, Shaye headed for the kitchen, setting a new pot of coffee and then just walking through the house. She needed to start putting her own touches there but had been reluctant to.

Hearing the doorbell, Shaye crept that way, staring out at the couple standing there. Opening the door, she welcomed Abe and Emma, Peter and his wife, Richard and Raleigh, and Don and Delanie. Hugs were given and returned before they mingled in the kitchen.

"You four couples are here?" Shaye was puzzled at that. She had not expected them.

"We are. First, we are here to support you both." Emma saw Slavin appearing in the kitchen, hunting for Shaye. "And then we want to go over what we have and then make some plans. If you are like us, you want to go on the offensive. We all did." Emma bit at her lip for a moment. "Only with Abe and I? I had a connection to a man who used to be in the mob. He left it as he became a Christian. His former friends stepped in to take out the threat to us."

"He did that? Of course, he would. You were family to him for some reason, weren't you? You helped him in some way." Shaye studied Emma and then Abe. "Your father, Abe? He did too."

Abe and Emma shared a look. Not many people knew that history. Shaye had made a good guess that only could have come from God.

"It's true, Shaye. We can't share what happened but God has given you an understanding that not many people have." Abe held up a folder. "Now, let's find somewhere we can pray and then we work away at what we can do for you two."

Slavin shut the door after the couples late that evening. It had been refreshing to have someone other than family praying for them, someone who knew to a certain extent what they were facing. He felt Shaye beside him and simply wrapped her to him.

"Did we really make those plans?" Shaye's voice was subdued but held a tone of wonder.

"We did. And we will start implementing them tomorrow. Peter said his team will be around as will some of the other three teams. We are not on our own, my love. Never on our own." Slavin studied his bride before he kissed her.

"No, we are never alone. God has promised that He will never leave us or forsake us. He wants us to go on with the life that He has planned for us. It's just the getting there that will be difficult and dangerous." Shaye's eyes closed as she heard Slavin praying for them.

Chapter 36

Sean stared at his brother the next morning, dumbfounded at his words before he looked down at the paper that Slavin was waving at him. He caught it and read the names, fear growing within him at them.

"You're sure about this, Slavin?" Sean looked up at his brother, seeing the determination in him to end it all but also to protect his family.

"We are. Abe and Emma and the three other security team leads and their wives met with Shaye and I last night. This is who we suspect. Emma is working on proving it before she passes it on to Jerome and John. We are going to be out there, Sean. We are choosing life over what we have been living."

"I see. That makes it more dangerous for you." Sean frowned for a moment. "How does that affect the rest of us?"

"We don't think that you are in any danger. They want us, Shaye and I, or more particularly me. We know that Shaye was wanted by that man to set up phony estimations. That would never happen. This? It's deeper than what we thought and much more dangerous. The archives that I have been researching? We think it's just the tip of the iceberg and that there is something more that needs to be found. Only I haven't found it yet."

"Can we get together and work on that?" Sean was desperate to help his brother solve whatever this was that he was involved in.

———

"I think that's a good idea. We're meeting at our home tonight. And yes, Annie and Andrew are welcome. Shaye's setting up a bed just for him. She says he needs one at his uncle's home and asked why that had never been done before." Slavin grinned as he remembered the look on her face.

"Annie has asked that over the months. And it's about time. Andrew loves being with you." Sean walked away, lost in thought, not seeing his brother watching him. He prayed for Slavin and Shaye, knowing that they were just going to put themselves out there in some manner and that made it even more dangerous for them.

That late afternoon, Slavin's home felt full. He studied all the people who had gathered there, laughter sounding through the rooms as they found their meal and then a place to sit. He was glad that the living room was large. It held the whole group. Slavin turned as he felt an arm around him and just hugged Shaye to him.

"Will we accomplish anything?" Shaye was not so sure that they would. She was praying that way. "Where is God right now, Slavin?"

"God? He is here. He is sheltering us in the hollow. Covering us with His wings. Giving us peace and comfort that we shouldn't have and do have. We were prayed for all those years ago. We are His witness to those who are not His, to show them His love and understanding." Slavin's head rested against his beloved Shaye for a moment. "He knows who and what we are facing but He has already won against them. We just have to have the faith and trust that He will lead us to that person."

"And He will. I guess as humans we don't see that. We want to trust in ourselves. It's hard to let go of that." Shaye elbowed Slavin as he gave a low laugh.

"You're so right, my love. Now, let's find our meal, spend some time in prayer, and then start working on this."

The next morning, Slavin reached for Shaye's hand, leading her away from his vehicle and into the historical society building. Neither of them wanted to be there but they felt that they had no choice. Shaye was not going out on any estimations at present, feeling it was just too dangerous for her. Instead, she agreed to help Slavin with his research, thinking that might help them end whatever this was.

Slavin looked around at the pile of folders that he had been handed, sighing to himself. This was turning into a bigger investigation than he thought it would be. Someone was feeding the public wrong information and he wanted to correct that. He just didn't know who or why. That hadn't even been discovered despite John and Jerome digging into it.

Shaye raised her head just after what should have been their lunch hour. She frowned at Slavin for a moment before her hand touched his arm. Slavin jumped and then looked her way.

"Shaye?"

"I found something, Slavin." She shoved the folder over to him. "I've taken photos of it. I think this explains why. I don't know that you were to be given that information but you were. Someone here is working on your side, not with whoever it is." Shaye looked at the folder. "It has your name on it. That must mean that it's yours and you can take it with you."

Slavin nodded, the folder slipped into his briefcase, the other folders neatly piled together to return to the information desk. He walked from the building, Shaye's hand in his.

"Let's find a diner to have lunch, Shaye, and then we head for home. I don't feel safe out here today." Slavin shuddered for a moment. "On second thought, let's just head for home."

Shaye studied Slavin as she worked away on a meal for them. She frowned as he just sat and stared at the folder before she moved it to one side and then set his plate of food down before she was sitting beside him.

Slavin roused, his hand reaching for his lady's. He studied her in turn, seeing the stress and worry and even fear that she was trying hard to hide from him. He sighed. Lord, this would be a really good time to find out who this is and why. We can't take much more.

Their lunch finished, Slavin simply shoved their plates away from them before he wrapped his bride in his arms, his head bowing as he prayed. He begged for protection and answers for whatever it was. Neither of the couple moved for a long time, finding God's peace gradually working in their hearts.

———

Shaye raised her head at last, on her feet to refill their coffee cups. She sat back down, watching carefully as Slavin reached for the folder. She just knew that this would move the investigation along. Shaye was just afraid for what was yet to come. The unknown was what was weighing her down that day and she wanted to know the answers.

"Shaye? This was really in that pile?" Slavin didn't doubt it. He would just have to explain how he got it.

"It was, sweetheart. At the bottom of the pile. You hadn't got that far yet." Shaye studied him once more. "What had you found?"

"Not what we wanted to but what we thought that we would." Slavin was on his feet, heading for his briefcase and pulling his notes from it. He was back beside Shaye in no time, his notes dropping to the table. "This is where it gets really dangerous, my love. I don't want any harm to come to you."

"Or to you. And it will. It always does." Shaye reached for his hands. "Let's pray once more, sweetheart, before we start in on this. And I just know that your family and friends will want to be involved." She smirked at him as he laughed.

"That they will. Okay, prayer and then this."

Chapter 37

Slavin watched Shaye closely as she just sat, her hand on the folder. He wasn't sure what she was thinking but thinking deeply she was.

"Slavin? I glanced through this. It has names, dates, addresses, whatever." Shaye turned to him. "We can't investigate them all."

"No, we can't but Emma can." Slavin reached for the folder, surprised that it only held two pages. "There's not much here."

"No, not paper wise, but it likely has a wealth of information." Shaye was taking photos of the pages and then sending those photos on to Emma. "Emma has gotten back to me already." She was surprised at that. She frowned at the text message. "She has most of those names."

"She would have. No one, not even, Emma, can explain how she does that."

"That's what she said." Shaye's voice died away. She pointed at a name of a couple. "This couple, Slavin. I think this is who it is." Her finger was shaking as she spoke. "I've seen them around where I have been. And they shouldn't have been. They weren't buying or selling. And they're not estimators."

"No, they're not. No one seems to know where their finances come from." Slavin sent the name off to John and Jerome before he was back into his notes, pulling that information on the couple that he had found. "I found this on them today. They are involved in the historical society but not in a good way, I suspect."

"No, they wouldn't be." Shaye sat back. "Listen to me for a moment, Slavin. What if someone was doing this to the website, changing information to get you involved and then to have you find what is needed to bring them to justice? Is that possible?"

Slavin had already reached that conclusion. He simply wrapped his bride in a hug, his head resting on top of hers.

"I think that you're correct. God was impressing something like that on me this morning. It has never made sense for anyone to change what information is there."

Shaye was on her feet, retrieving a laptop and then bringing up the website.

"There has to be a clue in the information, then." She was printing off the information as Slavin was on his feet to retrieve it. "We go through it now, looking at it differently."

"We do, sweetheart. This should help to solve it." Slavin sighed as he heard the doorbell. "Were we expecting anyone?"

"Not that I know of." Shaye walked quietly that way, peeking out and then opening the door. Roane stood there, a smile on his face that didn't quite meet his eyes. "Roane? You're here. You have information."

"I do. I need to go over it with you both." Roane studied his friend. "But you have come to some conclusions."

"We have. And Slavin can explain it to you." Shaye stood where she could watch the two men, not that she wasn't welcome to join them. She just couldn't. She walked away to her prayer corner, finding solace and peace with her Abba Father. Shaye was on her feet thirty minutes later, heading to where she could hear voices.

Sean had appeared as had John. She hadn't heard the doorbell but that didn't bother her. What bothered her was that the two men were there.

"Sean? John? You have information to add. John? Aren't you to be working?" Shaye sat back down beside her groom, her eyes on the four men as they looked at one another and then her.

"I'm here as a friend, Shaye. Only as a friend. God sent me. Jerome's okay with that." John looked up at the ceiling for a moment before he looked straight at her. "Slavin says that you have named someone."

"I have." Shaye uttered the name as much as she didn't want to, not surprising John as she had suspected. "You've been looking into them."

"We have looked at everyone in the society. And yes, those are names that we have taken a deeper look at. I can't tell you why or what we found." John didn't look away from her, seeing her understanding of his words.

"Of course, you can't. It would compromise the investigation. And we can't have that. Not at all." Shaye reached for the new paperwork that had appeared and was lost in her reading, not hearing the conversation around her.

"Shaye? What did you discover?" Roane's hand rested on the paperwork for a moment.

"That we are in more danger than we were." Shaye was frightened and it showed. "Do you know how deep these people are into crime? Do you realize that they have been using the society to move false information around the area and likely across the province."

"That is what we have determined, Shaye. Now, we just have to prove what they are involved in." Roane turned to John. "Now, what do we do?"

"I take this information and head into the office." John's hand was waving. "I know. I'm off today but this is critical to the investigation. Jerome will need to see this." He was gathering up his documents and walking away.

Shaye followed him, stepping out on to the porch to watch him drive away. She studied the car parked across the street and nodded. Of course, someone would be there. Her phone was out as she called for a patrol vehicle to come and take that person away as she described it.

Late that night, Slavin stood in his office, his arm around Shaye. They had come to their conclusions and now needed to make some plans. Just what those plans were, neither were sure. All that they were sure about

———

was that they were not hiding. Not any more. That didn't solve anything, only prolonged it.

Shaye leaned against Slavin, drawing from his strength and peace. She had never expected to marry, not like they had, but she could not envision her life without him. She walked away at last, heading for her rest, hearing Slavin's footsteps as he walked through the house to ensure that it was locked up for the night. They were at a crisis, they both acknowledged, afraid of losing one another and of what was to come, but determined to end their adventure in the next few days.

Chapter 38

The next morning, Shaye opened the front door to stare at the man standing there. She slammed the door closed, locking it and then backing up into Slavin who had appeared behind her. He frowned at her and then peered through the window before he was reaching for the door.

"Breck? You're here?" Slavin reached to shake Breck's hand, closing the door after him. "Sweetheart, this is Breck. He works for the Barnabas Foundation. He's here for a reason."

Breck grinned, apologizing for scaring Shaye. That had not been his intention, not at all.

"I'm sorry. I know that I'm early but we have information that we wanted to get to you." He followed the couple as they moved to the kitchen. "I'm here before your breakfast."

"That's okay. You can join us if you haven't eaten." Slavin studied Shaye, seeing a brittleness in her that morning that hadn't been there. All he could do was pray for his lady.

"Breck? You had information for us?" Slavin's arm was around Shaye, keeping her in her chair, their breakfast finished and cleared away.

"I do. But before we look at it, we need to pray." Breck's head was bowed as he did just that, bringing them it seemed right into heaven. He looked up at last, watching the two. "As you know, all of us in the foundation went through some really hard and difficult times. We have been working on your adventure as we can." He tapped the folder in front of him. "This is what we have found. I did speak with Jerome last night and he has it. He asked that I go over it with you two."

"And you are here to do that." Shaye sighed. "Will this end it?"

"It will, Shaye. This is when it is a difficult and dangerous time for you both. We can't stick you away somewhere and pray that we find the couple. We need you two to be out there. I know that security teams are moving in as we speak."

"We have no life." Shaye's complaint caused the men to grin briefly. "As long as it's over in the next day or two, I can live with that."

"And if you don't, you might not live." Breck didn't pull his punches with Shaye. He knew that he couldn't, that she would accept nothing but the truth and all of that truth.

"No, we might not even survive with the teams. That's how life works, isn't it?" Shaye sat back, watching Breck and knowing that he wanted to talk to them. There was just a hesitation in his manner that she was picking up on. "What are you unsure about?"

Breck grinned at her. This lady was good at reading people, he thought, just who Slavin needed in his life.

"We have done our best to track this person. That person is hiding and hiding deep in your town. We want to keep you two safe, but you're out and about, just like we all were." Breck had briefly shared with Shaye the stories of the men associated with the Barnabas Foundation. She had been shocked, to say the least, to hear of the life and death adventures that they had had.

"Okay. We realize that." Shaye was at the point where she really didn't care anymore if someone found them. In fact, she wanted that. Then just maybe this whole thing would be over. She had left that burden with her Lord but it was weighing heavily on her that morning. "How do we do this? And just what do you have?"

Breck grinned at her again, his eyes studying first Shaye and then Slavin. He nodded to himself. They were ready to go on the offensive, there was no doubt about that. Every couple did at some point.

"What we found? Slavin, someone is trying to help you. By bringing you in to delve into the changes on the website, this person has ensured that whatever is going on will be looked at. That we have determined. The changes will revert back to the original from what we have discovered once the responsible party is found and arrested."

"It's strange, Breck. Could they not have gone to the police?" Slavin was still puzzled by it all, watching Shaye as her head began to shake.

"They're too close to the person, aren't they, Breck? If they went to the police, their life would be in danger. Doing this? They have ensured that someone else would look at it. Only, they didn't think that Slavin would have the danger that he is."

"More than likely, you are correct, Shaye." Breck didn't continue and add that Emma had already found that person and that person was tucked away somewhere safe.

Breck stayed for close to three hours, going over the material and then just praying once more for the couple. He was deeply troubled for them, knowing that this was coming up to the most dangerous time for them.

Shaye turned from the desk in the office. She had had enough of trying to sort through everything and just wanted it over. Slavin walked towards her, enveloping her into a tight hug, his head on hers. He was deeply afraid for his lady, afraid that whoever it was would find her and she would disappear or die. He had to leave that with God.

"Shaye? What do you want to do?" Slavin waited patiently for her to speak, knowing that she had to think through what she wanted. He knew that she wanted what he did, for this all to be over.

"I don't know, Slavin. I truly don't. If we're out and about, we bring danger to others. If we stay home, whoever this is, wins. And I am tired of him or her winning." Shaye leaned back to look up at him. "So, how be we make plans to flush this person out? Can we do that?"

"We can. Peter sent a text. He, Richard, and Don want to meet with us tonight if they can and bring Abe in on a conference call. They want to help end this by making plans that we may or may not like."

Slavin grew quiet, more worried than he cared to admit to.

"I see. So we make plans and then implement them. I'm scared, Slavin. I am so scared." Shaye blinked back the tears that clouded her vision. "And I am so afraid that I'll lose you."

"I am as well, my love. God is here. He has gone before. He allows nothing to come near us that is not in His will for us. We forget that God is in control." Slavin turned them towards the living room, seating Shaye and then coming back with their coffees. "We'll pray it through, my love. Now, are you working today at all?"

Shaye shook her head. She wasn't at present. In fact, she was not sure that she would ever go back to that work. It was something that she and Slavin needed to discuss. Shaye felt too vulnerable when she was out there and that had changed what her plans were for her life.

Chapter 39

Seated in their office that night, Shaye was as close to Slavin as she could sit. Her eyes were on the three men who had appeared even as she heard them greeting Abe. Their conference to end their adventure had begun. Shaye just didn't know if the plans that would evolve would work that way. She could only pray that it did. She was not surprised when all heads were bowed and the men prayed for the couple. Shaye had come to expect that from them.

Raising his head, Slavin looked around the room. This was it, he thought. Please, Lord, let us plan and implement those very plans to bring glory to You but also to end this, whatever this is. We can't continue as we are. We're wearing out and need to be free of whoever it is.

"Slavin. Shaye. What do you want to do?" Richard spoke first. The four security team leaders had already conferenced among themselves, plans in place. They had more than one that they wanted to present but it was up to the couple if any of the plans went forward.

"We want this over, Richard. How do we do that? I know that this person is out there, watching us wherever we are. We can't go on properly with our lives with the threats hanging over us and those around us."

"No, you can't." Don spoke up. "So, here are some plans. We met and came up with some ideas.

For now, that is what they are. Ideas. It is up to you to agree to any of them or come up with some new ones." He watched as Shaye waved a paper at him. "Shaye? Your plans?"

"They are. We decided to come up with some and then have you go over them. Let's see how close our plans are to yours." Shaye grinned at him as he laughed, knowing exactly what she was doing. She was trying to bring a lightness to the room. Only, she won't sure if that would work.

"Okay, let's see what you have." Don was on his feet, making copies for them all before he was back in his chair, reading through the papers. She was good, he decided, both of them are. Her plans just might work. They followed closely to what the four men had come up with. "You're good, you two. Now, let's plan."

An hour later, plans had been discussed and then approved. It meant more danger for the couple but they had come to expect that. Those plans would start on the next day. Richard simply bowed his head and prayed for them, the others following his lead.

The next morning, Shaye stared at Slavin who was staring back at her. They had spent the night in prayer, not sleeping, and just waiting on their Abba Father. They had confidence that their plans were His but it still worried and scared them, what they had decided to do. They had no way of knowing just how that person would react. That was the unknown of it all.

The couple walked towards the park near their home. This was their first stop of the day. They didn't know how many stops would be required, but they were determined to hit all the spots and places that they had decided on for that day. If the person responsible had not been drawn out that day, then they were prepared to go to the next day's list and continue until they had succeeded. They just didn't know how long it would take or how much it would take from them. That was the problem.

Slavin's hand gripped Shaye's tight in his as they walked their planned walks through the day, into and out of stores, the library, the grocery store for their weekly food run, the diner for a meal out, and then finally to lock themselves away in what they prayed was safety in their own home. No one could guarantee that they would be safe. That much had been emphasized to them.

Roane and Nickol had appeared not long after they arrived home, bags of food in hand. None of them felt much like eating, particularly Shaye. They knew that this was where it became so dangerous for them.

"Roane? You have something to talk to us about?" Slavin's arm was around Shaye as they found seats in the living room.

"I do. Did you see anyone out there today?" Roane watched them closely. He has spoken with Richard and Peter and knew that those two men had been watching the ones following the couple.

"Not off hand. I don't have training in that." Shaye was angry and her words were bit out. "We were out there. I could feel someone watching us."

"You were. Both Richard and Peter commented on who they saw. You were protected today, guys. Some of the men and, yes, women were arrested on outstanding warrants. You're back out tomorrow?"

"We are. We want this over. I can't work while this is going on. I don't know if I will ever feel safe to go back to what I chose as a career." Shaye was saddened at that but anxious to see what else that she could do with her training.

"We know that." Nickol reached for a folder that he had dropped to the table beside him. "This is what happened over the day. I spoke with Peter and yes, I was out there too. I worked with one of Peter's men."

"You were? Roane?" Slavin's eyes slid closed as Roane nodded. "Thank you. Now, what do you have?" Slavin's hand reached for the folder, opening it and then reading through the paperwork inside. He frowned at the couple that Roane and Nickol had named. "This couple?"

"That's correct, Slavin. It's about you but not about you. They are hitting at you to take you down. If they discredit you and your work, then whatever you have done in the past or are working on now is suspect. John and Jerome are tracing them back to one of the cases that you worked on. They are appealing the verdict right now and if they discredit you, then the case is tossed." Roane watched Slavin closely, seeing how tight Shaye had moved to her groom.

Slavin's face paled as he realized the ramifications of what Roane was saying. That made everything come into clear focus.

"It makes sense, you know. But Shaye?" Slavin looked down at his bride.

"Her case seems to be separate from you. But there is a link. The person arrested for going after Shaye? He's cousins with this couple."

Slavin and Shaye stared at each other. They were connected after all. They had just not expected it to be in this way.

Chapter 40

Early the next morning, Shaye was on her feet, heading for their research. Something was just not making sense to her and she was determined to find out why. Sitting back at last, her face was white. It wasn't that couple after all. It was their family. And that made is more difficult as there were a number who could be after them. Her phone was out as she sent text messages to John, Jerome, Richard, Peter, and then Roane. Shaye paused and raised her head as she heard a noise outside. Creeping through the house, she watched the men standing on the driveway. She didn't know them but the streetlight clearly showed their features. Shaye's camera was up as she took pictures of the men.

Slavin stood for a moment behind Shaye before he was wrapping her in his arms. A small squeak came from her before she leaned back against him. His hand reached for her phone as he studied the men.

"I know these men, Shaye. They're from a security team, Don's and Abe's in fact. They're with us today. Richard told us yesterday that these two men might walk in today to help." Slavin gave a small grin as the grumpy look on her face.

"He did. They should have warned us that they would be here." Shaye stalked towards the door, opening it before Don or Abe had a chance to knock. "Could you not have come at a decent hour? It's just dawn." She spun and walked away, leaving Slavin shaking his head at her, a huge grin on his face.

Abe and Don shared a look, not quite sure what they had walked into. The door closed behind them as Slavin pointed towards the office.

"In there, fellows. I think Shaye has discovered something that we need to discuss." Slavin walked that way, Abe and Don trailing after him. "What did you discover, my love?" He reached for the papers that Shaye was thrusting at him. "The families?"

"That's right. The families. Someone sent me a text really early this morning and that started off the search. The couple aren't involved in this." Shaye was sober as she spoke.

"That's what Emma has picked up on." Abe handed over the envelope that he held. "This is what she has discovered. How be we go over it and then adjust any plans for today? I assume that you two will be out there again."

"We will be, Abe. We want this over. The families are hiding." Slavin frowned for a moment. "John was in touch yesterday. They have arrested some people. I wonder if they were family members."

Abe and Don shared a look. John had confirmed with the four team leaders that the couple's families were being arrested. They just had to keep Slavin and Shaye safe until they were all in custody. And that would be difficult, given how the couple wanted to be out there.

"What are your plans for today?" Don stared at the paperwork before he glanced at Shaye. He frowned and thought how brittle she was at that point in time. "We need to pray for you two. God is here. He is in control. He has you covered with His hand and is protecting you. We just need to keep you safe for the next few days.”

“The next few days?” Shaye stared at him. “I want it over today.”

“And it might be, Shaye. God’s timing is perfect. It will be over when it’s over. We can’t rush into this. John and Jerome are working frantically to solve it but they have other cases they are investigating.”

Shaye was on her feet, pacing away from the office. She found a seat on the side of the bed, wrapping her arms around herself. She didn’t want to surrender this burden to the Lord. She wanted to be the one solving it. Only that likely would not happen. And she had to accept that.

Slavin watched her before he spoke, not taking his eyes from the doorway.

“What do we do, guys? I want this over and without any more harm coming to Shaye. We’ve been receiving the text messages, the letters in the mail box, and a parcel with photos in the last couple of days. They have all been turned over to John and Jerome.” Slavin looked at the other men. “How do we end this and end this now without any injuries to us or someone around us?”

“That’s what we are here for, Slavin.” Don looked up at him, a frown on his face for a moment. “Do you have any idea who?”

Slavin nodded, simply stating the couple's names. The others in the room looked at him in shock before Peter was nodding. He had shown up not that long ago.

"It would be them. We've suspected for years that they are behind something. Whoever has been playing you with the website must have information and proof." Peter rubbed at his head. This was not going to be easy, he knew.

Slavin paced his office that night. He frowned as he thought through the information that had been provided to him and then the names. He shook his head. Slavin was not convinced that it was that couple. He reached for his phone and read the text from Emma, giving new names. He sighed. Shaye was correct and Emma had sent material confirming this. They now had to come up with a plan to catch that couple and he was not convinced that they could.

The next morning, Shaye was back into their home almost before he had risen. He stared at her and then behind her. She had been out and about town extremely early, her team following her.

"Where's your team?" He pulled her into the house, wrapping her into a hug and then kissing her.

"I ditched them. That couple is too savvy. They won't come at us if the guys are around." Shaye was convinced that this was true. "We need to find someone who isn't known here in town. Those four teams? They are. Who can we call?" Shaye was pacing, convinced that she was right.

Slavin stared at her, not sure he had heard her correctly before his phone began to chime. He read the text message before he passed the phone over to Shaye.

Shaye stared at the message and then at Slavin, hope on her face.

"They would do that?"

"They would. Abe's friends and his uncle and another retired officer are on their way. They will be joined by some officers from Oak City, Elmton, and Mistletoe. All we have to do is wait for an hour or so and then appear in the downtown area. The teams will be around but not close enough to be obvious that they are there." Slavin watched her to get her reaction, seeing her shrug.

"I guess, sweetheart. We don't have much to lose, do we?" All Slavin could do was reach to hug his lady and then walk away to compose himself.

Chapter 41

The next morning found Slavin and Shaye once more walking the downtown area. This time, they knew they had shadows but they could not see them. That scared them both but with a look at each other, they had set out on their trek for the day.

Slavin reached for a door handle, pausing as he did so before he was backing away. There had been such a strong sense of danger there that he could not even touch the door. Shaye stared at him and then frowned. She could feel the same danger and tugged Slavin with her.

The door opened and then closed as they walked away. They could hear the footsteps following them and picked up the pace of their walk. Now that it appeared their enemy was behind them, they were too scared to continue. Shaye could hear Slavin's audible prayer for protection and safety and also an end to what they were facing.

John and Jerome were behind the middle-aged man who strode along the almost empty sidewalk, trailing after Slavin and Shaye. They exchanged a glance. This was not the man who they were after. He worked for him and had been identified as a hitman. Just why a hitman was after either one of the couple was not quite clear. That was being worked on by other detectives. For now, Slavin and Shaye had just become a priority for them all.

———

212

Shaye tugged Slavin with her, disappearing into a small cafe and then heading out the back door through the kitchen. She was friends with the owner and had done that many times. Slavin hesitated for a moment before he shoved open the door and was running away, Shaye's hand tight in his. He looked for somewhere to hide but could not find anywhere until Shaye's hand pulled him towards an empty building. She was inside, one of the street people pointing to a room. Neither one knew that the man was an undercover police officer who had been approached by John to provide cover and a hiding place for the couple.

The man chasing them hit the alleyway despite the protests of the cafe staff that he couldn't be in the kitchen. He searched for the couple, not finding them. Turning, he froze for a moment, seeing the officers who were now surrounding him. Cuffed and searched, he was then shoved into a patrol vehicle.

John turned for a moment, catching the eye of the officer standing in the building doorway and gave a slight nod. He would track them down but for now, he was needed somewhere else.

Slavin appeared in an empty room in the building, Shaye tight to him before he gave a nod and walked away, heading for home. They had succeeded in what they had planned for the day. It was up to John, Jerome, and the others to complete what was needed for the arrest warrants and then serve them. They were heading for home.

Stepping back from his back door, Slavin reached to hug each of his family members who appeared, little Andrew clinging to his uncle. That little one refused to leave him until he saw Shaye and then almost threw himself at her. Shaye's face lit up as she cuddled the little boy, finding peace and comfort from his hugs and kisses.

"Is it over, son?" Stephen stood with an arm across Slavin's shoulders. He was asking the question that they all wanted an answer to.

"Just about, Dad. Just about. John called and said for us to stay inside today. They are preparing the warrants that they need to move in and arrest whoever it was." Slavin could feel the tension and stress leaving his body, almost causing him to collapse. "Thanks for your prayers, guys. That was what got us through."

"We could do no less." Emily reached to hug her son. "Now, we need to plan for when John and Jerome will be around to explain everything for us. We need to thank everyone." She spun as she heard Shaye begin to laugh. "Shaye?"

"Do you realize how many that will mean?" Shaye grinned at Emily began to laugh too. "We'll do a potluck, I think, Emily. That will save us a lot of work."

"That it will. Now, what do we do?" Emily walked through the house, seeing the little changes that Shaye was making in finding her place there. She turned as she heard footsteps.

Slavin approached his mother, hugging her. This had been a dangerous time for them all and stress levels had been high. God had protected them from most harm and was bringing their adventure to a halt.

"Mom? You're okay?" Slavin was worried about his mother for a moment.

"I'm fine, son. Go find your bride and then we'll spend some time in prayer and praise." Emily watched as he walked away to do just that. She thought back over the years from when he was a newborn to now and was proud of the man that God had led him to become. He was a light to everyone around him, choosing to live his life as God directed him.

A week later, John watched his friend carefully. He could see the change in Slavin now that he was no longer in danger. His attention turned to Shaye as she sat with some of the ladies who were becoming good friends. She needed that, he knew, and was glad that God had provided them for her, helping her to choose to live her life as He would want.

Slavin caught John's eye once more and then nodded. He slipped to a sitting position before his bride, an arm around her tucking her close. He knew that his father would want to spend time in prayer and for that, he was glad and grateful.

An hour later, they all looked up. Time had been spent in prayer and then just waiting on God's peace to flood each of them. John reached for his folder, Jerome nodding at him. It would usually be the senior detective who gave the details. This time? It was John. The new man on the squad would have a chance to explain everything to the couple and the family and friends who had gathered nearby. John gave a small smile as he watched little Andrew climb up on Shaye's knee and then settle back against her. It was obvious to everyone that she was special to the little guy.

"John? What can you tell us?" Slavin finally spoke, his eye on his friend.

"What can we tell you? A lot in fact." John looked around. "The man who followed you that day? He was the hitman, hired to bring you to the couple who were after you. He has been transferred to another jurisdiction where he is wanted for murder. God protected you that day by not allowing you into that store. He was waiting for you.

"Now, as to the couple? It was not who we expected at all. I think we all suspected someone on the historic society board. It wasn't at all. It was Terry and June Wightman." John paused as the comments flew around the room, shock uppermost in the words. "Yes, them. I know. They seemed to be up and up and supporting the town and all of the societies. In fact, they weren't. We have all heard about historical items disappearing. This was what they were up to. They would have someone steal an item and then sell it to the highest bidder, usually overseas or outside of Ontario. They didn't think that they would ever be caught. Adam Weaver who works for the society stumbled upon an email at one point that he should not have. We say it was God who did that. He has been the one changing what was on the website, praying that someone would figure it out. He did, I think, reach out to you, Slavin, without you knowing it was him. He has returned the website to what it was. Adam didn't feel that he could come to us without any proof. He was fortunate not to have been killed by them.

"The director of the historical board? He has been arrested for other crimes. He thought that you were on to him, Slavin. Shaye? Your comment about the insurance company dropping your coverage? That would never have happened as you were the victim, not the villain. It was their plan that you would work for them and not report them.

"Shaye? Your problems? They were behind them too. They thought that if you worked for them, then they would have access to the homes where they could steal historical items. They planned to kill you at some point and blame Slavin. How that was to be? They are not even clear on that themselves." John looked around. "I think that pretty much sums up what I can say until it all goes to court. And it will go to court. We have too much evidence against them."

A year later, Slavin went looking for Shaye, not seeing her in the house anywhere. He paused and then smiled, heading for the back deck and the little area that she had claimed for herself. He stood and watched her closely, seeing her head bent over the little bundle that she held.

Slavin slipped to a seating position beside her, arms around her, a kiss to her temple. Shaye looked up with a huge smile on her face. Both were happy and content. Having little Evan join their family just a couple of weeks prior had completed the family.

"Okay, my love?" Slavin's finger came out to touch his son's hand, finding little fingers curling tight around it.

"I am, sweetheart. I am. I am so thankful that the trials are behind us. We can now go forward with the life that we have chosen and that God chose for us." Shaye settled back against Slavin.

"God has been good and gracious, sweetheart. That He has. And with little Evan here? We're stronger and more sure of ourselves as people and now as parents. We don't have to fear anyone trying to harm us." Slavin grew quiet. He had spent time with John that morning, just touching base with him about the investigation and its closure.

"That we are." Shaye's eyes dropped to her son, watching as he slept. She had never planned to marry, had never planned to be a mother, but God had chosen a different life for her than she had expected to live.

"Mom and Dad want to have us for dinner, Shaye." Slavin waited for her to nod. "They have taken you in as a daughter, just as they did with Annie. They always wanted a girl."

"I am so grateful for them. I left my home when I was sixteen. I never heard from my parents after that. Emma looked into them. They were killed in a road accident when I was eighteen. No one knew where I was to inform me. I don't know if I would have ever reconciled with them."

"And Emma just let you know today?" Slavin's arms tightened around his lady. "I'm sorry, my love. I'm sorry that you didn't have the relationship with them that you needed."

Shaye shrugged. It was how her life had always been with them. She had been told many times that she was unwanted and unloved. Emma had put her in touch with the lawyer who had been looking for her. There were items and documents and a fund that needed to come to her. They just had not been able to find her.

"I love you, Shaye." Slavin kissed his lady before he just settled back on the wicker loveseat, content with how his life was going. Shaye had decided not to work outside of the home and they were content with that.

"I guess we need to move, don't we?" Shaye made no effort to do just that. It was a warm night, little Evan was asleep, and she was held by the man who loved and adored her and whom she loved and adored in return. Her eyes sought the sky, watching as dusk settled down on them, a prayer of thankfulness raised to her Heavenly Father. He had led and protected them in ways that they had not even been aware of until it had come out in court. The couple were looking for some way to reach out to others. That would come as they grew in their faith, that much they were aware of.

Dear Readers:

Thank you for picking up the first book in a new series, *In His Choosing*. *Choosing Life* was not one that I ever expected to write but God had other plans. It has been my Nanowrimo challenge for November, 2024.

Slavin and Shaye chose to live life instead of hiding away from it and allowing evil to triumph. What do you face in your life that would have you choosing to live the life that God has planned for you? I know my life would not have been what I would have chosen, but God has chosen to bless me in ways that I didn't expect as I walk forward on the path He ordained for me.

Now, my characters are notorious for being unruly and dragging in multiple people from multiple books. Richard and his team are in *His Protectors*. Don and his team are in *His Defenders*. Abe and his team are in *His Guardians*. Jacob Whitson and he ones from Mistletoe are *Mistletoe Treasures*. Peter and his team appear in *Riley*. Breck and those from the Barnabas Foundation are in *The Barnabas Chronicles*. Doug and Darci are in *The Heart of a Lion*. Samuel and Noah are from *His Warriors*. Frankie is *Hidden in the Hollow*. Richard refers to Riley, who is *Riley*.

Thank you for reading this book. May God richly bless you as you traverse this journey called Life, waiting on His leading and guidance as we do so.

Ronna

9 781999 882159